THE CALL OF
JEREMIAH MCGILL

THE CALL OF
JEREMIAH MCGILL

JOSEPH MOORE

gatekeeper press

Tampa, Florida

The Call of Jeremiah McGill

Published by Gatekeeper Press
7853 Gunn Hwy, Suite 209
Tampa, FL 33626
www.GatekeeperPress.com

FIRST EDITION
Front and back cover designed by Dorothea Taylor

ISBN (paperback): 9781662919350
eISBN: 9781662919367

Acknowledgment -

I first would like to acknowledge God, Jesus, and the Holy Spirit. Thank you for trusting me with this precious gift, wrapped in a novel for all the world to embrace. To my Mother, Sanfort Moore, Father, Joseph Moore Jr., and family near and far, you inspired me to write this book. To Apostle JoAnn McCauley and my church family, House of Prayer, the wonderful stories and tales you shared about our history put that spark in my writing. Meghan Moore, thank you for believing in the vision and giving it legs. Dorothea Taylor, your artistic talent is amazing. To Nancy Lohr, Louise Morris, Elizabeth Nowak, Lauren Crouch and so many other Beta Readers; thank you for the constructive feedback to make this project stronger.

To all the young and young at heart, I pray this book will lead you down the right path. Jesus tells us in his word that he will never leave us nor forsake us. I firmly believe that He is the answer to the problems you may be facing.

Look up and remember, He is soon to come.

Dedication -

This novel is dedicated to my brother, Terrence Ladell Lane. You may be absent in body to be present with our Lord and Savior, but you will never be forgotten.

CHAPTER 1

SUMMER HEAT OF '71 FINDS HEADLESS MOE

One Saturday afternoon, me and my buddies were sitting outside on my front porch enjoying some of Mama's ice-cold sweet tea she made for us to combat the heat. It seemed as if our town, Cape Creek, Missouri, had the heat and the humidity worse off. Folks stayed inside their homes with fans on, probably sipping on some iced lemonade while doing much of nothing.

"I'm tellin' y'all," Rodney started as we were finishing our last glasses of sweet tea. Tall, skinny, Rodney had just turned twelve and felt as if he was the leader of us, since he was the oldest.

"Ever since the beginning of the summer, I heard some strange things been going down where Headless Moe be at the train station."

The mysteries of paranormal activity that surrounded Headless Moe was all Rodney talked about that afternoon. I adjusted my thick, owl-like glasses, sitting perfectly on my dark brown skin as Rodney, who wasn't getting the satisfaction he wanted by us responding, decided to beef up the tension to his so-called "news."

"I overheard my mama talking to one of her friends, who said that one of our neighbors saw a headless ghost, staring right at 'em."

"You jivin', man!" responded a now curious and yet skeptical Drew. Drew was a bronze-skinned, heavier-set fellow that looked older than his age. He was not one who was fond of ghost stories and felt as if Rodney was just pulling someone's leg.

"You know you jivin', ain't ya? Ain't no Headless Moe."

Rodney swirled his glass around with a devious look on his face. "I wish I was, Drew. I wish I was."

One thing about Rodney I've learned from knowing him is that you never can figure out if he's telling the truth. He uses this skill as bait, making a story seem so good and believable that one would think he's telling you something real. Once hooked, he draws you in as his prey.

"Na-na-naw, it . . . it . . . it . . . it . . . can't . . . b-b-be," Drew stuttered, trying his best not to show any fear. "Th-th-th-there ain't no . . . su-su-such things as . . . as . . . ghosts, is there, Otis?"

"Now what ya askin' him for, Drew?" questioned Rodney. "What could Otis possibly know more than me?"

"I just don't believe you, that's all," answered Drew. A long silent pause drew out as Drew then turned towards Otis. "You don't believe what Rodney's tellin' us, do ya, Otis?"

Otis, who was rocking back and forth on the porch banister, stared at the golden-red sun. His perfect Afro hair gleamed, and his skin reflected the sunlight as it made his generally high yellow color become a golden-brown.

He looked at Drew and shrugged his shoulders. "I dunno. It is kind of hard to believe in such a thing as a headless ghost."

"See Rodney," Drew replied, happy that Otis backed him up. "Otis don't believe you either."

Rodney rolled his eyes, wiping sweat off his brow and face with nothing to say. No comeback. No smart remark to keep this Headless Moe tale alive.

Before us, the grayish-blue sidewalk of my house stretched until it met the metal gate. On the other side of it was Daddy's blue station wagon, or what I called the Blue Stallion. I stared at it and began thinking about tomorrow, another Sunday filled with church.

My father, Reverend Walter McGill, is the Pastor, with my mother as the choir director and my big brother Zeke as the organist. Daddy always said that we were born into greatness and that our family is called. Seems everyone, except me, knew who they were. Me? I wasn't anything but just an eleven-year-old Pastor's Kid. A PK, as some call it.

"Man, this ain't cool," Rodney suddenly said.

He stood up where he was, on the second step of the porch, and leaped all the way to the middle of the sidewalk. "Y'all, let's do something."

"Something like what?" I asked.

"I don't know, Jeremiah," Rodney responded. "But it has to be something adventurous!"

Oh, great. Whenever we hear something about an adventure, that means a trick or prank is up the road. I didn't like it when we went on one of Rodney's adventures. We always end up in deep trouble or something goes terribly wrong with no plan, just Rodney trying to dominate.

"Whatchu got planned, Rodney?" demanded Drew.

"Well," replied Rodney. He stared at the sidewalk tiles one by one trying to keep the suspense going, which got on my nerves.

"Come on, Rodney. What's on your mind?" Otis asked dryly.

"We're going down to that old train station and look for Headless Moe."

"Oh no!" I jumped up, almost knocking my glasses off my face as I protested Rodney's idea of an adventure. "We can't be going down there, it ain't right!"

Rodney, who wasn't into my reasoning for not doing this adventure, side-eyed me and said, "Aww, quit being a square, Jeremiah. It ain't like anyone down there."

"I'm with Jeremiah," said Drew. "I think we should go down to the Nelsons' and get us a soda."

"You jokin', right, Drew?" Rodney said. "You rather think about food than go on an adventure of a lifetime?"

Although still scared, Drew reluctantly agreed to tag along. Otis seemed to be in too. I was still trying any tactic to call this whole thing off.

"But we still can't just walk on private property like that," I argued. "It's too hot and we can get lost. And may I remind you that I have a curfew?"

"Welp, y'all, looks like Jeremiah is at it again!" Rodney concluded. He was making those noises you would hear on police cars, saying that I was trying to stop their fun. Otis chuckled a bit, while Drew let out a big laugh. I saw nothing funny about Rodney's joke.

"You can't stay out late anyway because you're a *preacher's kid*," Rodney said to me. He knew I hated that name and always used it to get under my skin. "Besides, you too scared."

"I ain't scared," I exclaimed. I stood up and was walking down the edge of the bottom step where Rodney was with my chest sticking out, showing my bravery.

"So, you in?" Rodney said.

I became silent. Dead silent as I felt my conscience begin talking to me.

"See, what I tell you?" Rodney smirked. "Nothing but a scaredy preacher's kid."

"What's going on out there?"

The front door of our blue-and-white painted house opened. Mama, who was wearing a light green sundress with a sunflower, stood at the front screen door.

"Rodney, what in the world are you doing down there making all that noise?" she asked. She opened the screen door and stepped outside. Her smooth, light pecan skin accented the green and yellow colors of her dress. "You ain't sugar high, are ya?"

"No, Mrs. McGill," Rodney responded.

Mama looked around the porch at all the empty glasses. "Looks like y'all finish up the last of the sweet tea pretty fast, didn't y'all?"

"Yes, ma'am, and it was very good, too," replied Drew. Whenever Drew gets around Mama, it seems as if he turns on this southern-boy charm.

"Why, thank you, Drew. That's so sweet of you."

He smiled, showing his two front teeth, the right one chipped.

"I thought I heard y'all talking about going down to that abandoned train station?" Mama began questioning, standing at akimbo.

"No, Mrs. McGill, we weren't talking about that at all," Rodney quickly answered, lying hard to my mama.

"Good, y'all don't need to be going to that place."

I stared over at Rodney, who had his face down, trying not to listen to what Mama told us. "Lord Jesus, I don't remember being this hot since I was a little girl."

"Really, Mrs. McGill?"

"Yes, Drew, it's been that long. This kind of heat will have people's minds see things that ain't really there." She stopped, rubbed her brow full of sweat, then rubbed her smooth, relaxed hair flowing to her shoulder. "Otis."

Otis was still and quiet, not saying a word this whole time like he always did.

"Otis, how have you been doing lately?"

"Fine," he shyly answered while looking down at the sidewalk.

"Come closer, let me take a good look at you," she exclaimed.

Otis did what she asked, walking from where he was toward her.

"My, my, my," she started. "Boy, you've grown up, aren't you? I thought to myself when I saw you with your mama and little Sam in church last Sunday, that you becoming a handsome young man wearing your light brown pants with your white shirt. Your mother told me that you all received a letter from your brother Kenny this past week."

"Yes, ma'am, we did," Otis replied.

In the conversation that followed, I began thinking about that summer when Otis's oldest brother, Kenneth Wilson, Jr. was being called to serve in Vietnam. That was a sad day, watching him ship out along with many others around here fighting for what some called a senseless war. I didn't know if it was a senseless war or not at the time, but I couldn't imagine how Otis felt daily without his oldest brother. Three years later, even though he rarely talks about it, you can see the bravery he shows for his mother and his little brother, Samuel.

Mama nodded her head and smiled when Otis finished talking about the letter.

"Well, I know it's good to hear from him, and I will continue to pray for his safety. Tell your mother I'll be stopping by sometime today when it cools down."

"Yes, ma'am."

Mama collected all the glasses we used to drink our tea and the pitcher and walked to the door.

"If y'all do anything, you make sure you be careful! This heat ain't anything to play with and don't y'all be straying too far, ya hear?"

We all let Mama know that we understood what she told us.

"Can I get the door for you, Mrs. McGill?" Drew asked.

"No, Drew, that's OK, I got it. Jeremiah? You make sure you be back here before the streetlights come on, hear?"

"Yes, Mama."

While Rodney and Drew left my house and went searching for the Headless Moe, I made the decision to go with them. There was no way I was going to let Rodney have the best of me.

Otis lagged behind, trying to reason with me. "You know you don't have to go, Jeremiah," he said. "Personally, I still think Rodney may be making this Headless Moe story all up."

I thought so too and knew going along wasn't the best idea either.

"Lord knows I don't want to get in trouble," I responded. "Why did Rodney have to call me a preacher's kid, anyway?"

"Man, Jeremiah, you know how Rodney is. He's just trying to get to you. Besides, we all know the reason you're going is to prove that you're brave."

I often asked myself why I, a son of a preacher, had a friend like Rodney. Maybe it was because his family sometimes attended our church. It could be because our fathers were classmates. None of those things matter. What mattered was me proving to myself and Rodney that I was no scaredy preacher's kid.

CHAPTER 2

RODNEY'S LATEST PRANKIN'

This is how it all went down. When me and Otis made it to the old train station, we found Drew standing outside. He told us that Rodney was already inside, leaving us to *have* to go looking for him. Go figure.

The small, framed building was abandoned, left untouched like a forgotten time period. The grass around the building and tracks was a dry brown color, which added little life to the already decaying railroad tracks.

Drew clung to my shirt. "You see anything yet?" he asked.

"No," I said. "Not yet." I ripped his hand off my shirt and he shot a nervous glance.

"Well, we been down here, looked all around. I say let's go home."

"Not so fast, Drew," Otis said. "Rodney's down here somewhere. We need to find him. Something doesn't seem right about this whole thing."

Inside was just like the outside: bare, with dust and cobwebs all over the place. The whole area was lit dimly by the fading sun outside. The sound of its creaky front door greeted us when Otis jogged it. He took the first steps inside, with Drew following right behind him. I was a slight distance behind, worried about the streetlights coming on.

"OK, y'all," Otis started as he squatted down to draw out the plan. "We have enough light to check these rooms and find where Rodney went."

"Each room?" said Drew. "In this place?"

"Come on, Drew, we'll still be together."

"But what if something happens?" asked Drew, doubtful.

"Nothing is going to happen to you, Drew. You know I'll look out for you. Ain't no ghost gonna get us. I can promise that."

After all my years of knowing Otis, I still to this day can't figure him out. Although he was one of those kids that was quiet, meek, and soft-spoken, he was more poised and composed than any eleven-year-old I knew, like Superman.

We made our way to a swinging wooden door right across from the front entrance. As Otis pushed the door open, a glimmer of light caught our eyes in a room that could've been a kitchen at one point. No one was in here.

Otis gave us the signal as we made our way back to the main front of the station. There was no sign of Rodney.

"Jeremiah, you and Drew check that door beside the kitchen." Otis pointed as we followed him. "I'll check down this hall."

As Otis made his way down the long hallway, me and Drew approached another door and opened it.

"Yuck, this room smells vicious!" Drew expressed as we both covered our noses to what was the bathroom.

We agreed to look inside quickly and meet Otis down the hall before we died from the smell of mildew.

As Drew searched through the sink, I followed the strong foul stench in the air to the bathtub. The smell grew stronger as I peered over the bathtub with a reddish-brown ring circling around. There was a white sheet covering up something.

"Drew, something is inside this bathtub," I whispered, signaling for him to come over.

"Wh-wha-what do . . . do . . . you . . . th-think it . . . is?"

"I don't know."

Drew grew more frightened, as did I.

"Do . . . do . . . you . . . th-th-think we . . . should li-lift the sheet?"

I looked over at him, backing away slowly, then looked back at the thing in the bathtub.

"We're gonna have to."

"Well, let's find Otis first," Drew said. I agreed.

Suddenly, not a second after we turned around, I heard moaning and groaning sounds.

"The ghost of Headless Moe!" Drew gasped.

Right in front of us, that thing turned from a lifeless sheet laying in the bathtub to a shadow like a man with no head standing up. It had one foot out of the bathtub and both hands holding some weapon that looked like an ax. Drew and I stood there as a wind of death rushed right past my body. When the moans and groans got louder and more agitated, my whole body cringed with fear.

"OTIS!" Drew called as he backed slowly towards the door. "The GHOST OF HEADLESS MOE!"

My mind said run, but my body just stood there like the idiot it was. I gulped as I picked up my heavy legs one at a time and fell towards the bathroom door. As I quickly headed out the door, Drew wasn't with me. He was still standing at that same spot, shaking like a leaf.

"Drew," I shouted. "Drew, run!"

No use. When I opened the door, I saw Otis dash down the hallway like an Olympic track star.

"Drew is still in there," I said, panicking. "We gotta get him."

Otis said nothing but made his way to save Drew.

I grabbed his arm. "Are you crazy? That Headless Moe man is in there, a ghost with an ax." If Otis's plan was to fight this ghost one-on-one, then he was crazier than I thought. "We need a plan to get Drew out," I reasoned. "There's no time to fight that thing in there."

"Jeremiah, this ain't Headless Moe."

He opened the door and I followed right behind him. The so-called ghost was standing in front of Drew, who was down on his hands and knees, begging for mercy.

"Alright, Rodney," Otis said as he lifted Drew up. "The joke's over."

When the moaning and groaning sounds turned into familiar laughter, my fear boiled quickly into anger. This was not the Headless Moe we'd heard about.

"Rodney," I cried. "Why, you dirty dog."

Rodney laughed hysterically as he came out from the sheet he was under. The supposed ax was a pointed rock tied to a big stick he must have made up outside somewhere.

"Rodney?" Drew finally said as he slowly stood up. "Rodney, it's you?"

"Got y'all good, didn't I?"

"You were Headless Moe, Rodney?" Drew was still in the aftershock of the whole thing, trying to wrap his head around it.

"You should have seen your face, Drew, while you were screaming for help," Rodney cracked. "It was priceless. And you getting down on your hands and knees begging for mercy. Just like Scooby-Doo!"

"Enough, Rodney," Otis silenced. "You and your jokes caused enough trouble for one day."

"Come on, Otis," Rodney started, talking in that slick, sly voice that's his way of apology. "Y'all know I'm just playing."

No one said anything.

"Y'all know I'm just playing, right? It was all a prank."

"Yeah, yeah. We know it was your little prank," I said, slightly forgiving him.

"Well, I ain't so sure if it was a prank," Drew said. "You scared us and that ain't funny."

"Come on, Drew. It was all a joke, I promise. There is no Headless Moe," Rodney walked over to Drew, sticking out his hand, waiting for Drew's blessing to be his friend again. "We still tight, right?"

With Drew forgiving all, it left me wondering how Rodney slicked his way out of that prank. That wasn't the only thing on my mind.

It was dark outside with the streetlights coming on.

CHAPTER 3

SPEECH NUMBER 82:
THE PREACHER AND HIS SON

I tried to convince Mama that it wasn't my fault for missing curfew. Of course, she wasn't buying it, as she did not give me a chance to say anything. She just sent me straight to my room and told me that daddy was going to talk to me, after church. My face could've fallen to the floor. Listening to daddy lecture me was the worst thing that could happen.

All throughout Sunday morning service, my mind was preoccupied. While I usually take note and observe the saints praising God and speaking in tongues, I thought about the many speeches my old man could give to me. I think I counted to 119. I can just hear number 82 in my mind, the mother of all speeches that I proudly call "The Preacher and His Son."

"Jeremiah, you and Ezekiel are a representation of me and this family," he would say. *"You need to make us proud. You are the son of a preacher."*

Boy, I hated that speech to its core.

"Jeremiah?"

When service was over, most people were congregating outside, talking about the latest in the Vietnam War. I was sitting in one of the pews near Zeke and the organ. He was talking to a couple of girls in awe of his musical talents and knew he really didn't want to see his eleven-year-old brother. I must've interrupted his conversation with both girls leaving, but not before one of them gave Zeke a piece of paper with her phone number. He put the piece of paper in his pocket and sat beside me.

"Jeremiah, what are you doing over here?"

"I was waiting for you."

"Yeah, waiting on me and trying to be in my conversation," he said in disbelief, putting me in one of his playful brotherly headlocks.

I always found it kind of cool having a big brother like Zeke. It's like outside he's just a regular fifteen-year-old full of charm and popularity that sometimes hates having the responsibility of his eleven-year-old younger brother. Other times, especially when he's behind the organ, he turns into this maestro who knows the sounds and keys, and rhythms like no one I ever heard of. I swear he becomes a different person, almost like a genius.

"Service was packed this morning, wasn't it?" Zeke asked.

"Uh-huh."

"And Ma, with the choir, sounded good," he commented. "Pop was really in the spirit today, wasn't he?"

"Yeah," I agreed. "At least you ain't getting in trouble and have to go talk to him."

Zeke smiled a bit at my misery. "Aww come on li'l bro, it's not all bad. I've been in trouble plenty of times before and got punished by Pop."

"You have?" I asked, even though we both knew the answer to that.

"No, not really," he replied. "You're on your own on this one. I know Ma wasn't too happy when she was telling Pop about you missing curfew when he came home."

"But it's not all my fault, Zeke. I mean, how come our curfew is when the streetlights come on? Drew's and Otis's curfew is nine o'clock. Rodney has a curfew of eleven."

"Man, you know Ma and Pop run our house like a tight ship," Zeke reminded me. "Pop always says we aren't like other people."

I always wonder what it would be like being someone else, you know, just a regular kid. A kid who didn't have to go to church all the time. A kid who didn't have to obey a lot of rules.

"Whatever the case may be, they practically talked about you all night," Zeke then said. "You lucky they didn't have your hide last night."

"I'd rather take that," I said.

Our brotherly time was over when Zeke's best friend, Clint, yelled out. He was going for a drive in his car and wanted Zeke to ride shotgun. I was then left alone, waiting to walk the green mile.

***

"Jeremiah," I heard Daddy call.

I closed the door to his office behind me and walked up slowly to the desk filled with papers, pamphlets, offering envelopes, and a black-and-white picture of my great-grandfather, Elder Johansson McGill. Daddy was sitting behind the desk looking dead at me, not moving, not blinking once, with his hands clasped together. He just stared down at me.

"Have a seat, son. I want to talk to you."

I sat down slowly.

"Did you like the message that was preached?" he asked.

"Yes, sir," I replied.

"What did you like most about it?" He opened his big white Bible in front to some random page and just started reading while I thought of an answer.

"I liked the part about the sinner man turning to God and that Jesus loves us," I said, making that completely up on the spot.

"Jeremiah, your mother told me . . ." He stopped himself, closed the book he was reading, took off his glasses, and set them in front of him. "That you were late getting home yesterday."

I looked down at his glasses, then back at him.

"Is this true?" he asked me.

"Yes, sir."

I slumped in my seat a little as Daddy leaned forward towards me, then followed with an "I see. You want to tell me why?"

"I guess I didn't see the streetlights come on...sir," I replied.

"Ahh . . . I see. You know this is the third time this week that you've been late coming home."

He stood up, placed his glasses back on his face and walked around the desk to a nearby shelf, reached to the middle and grabbed two books from the center. As he carried those two books back to his seat and sat down with his eyes focused on me, I started sweating bullets on my palms.

"Now, tell me, why were you late this time?"

That's when I started singing like a canary.

"Well, it was Rodney's idea that we go see if there really is such a thing as Headless Moe down at the station because of all the rumors he supposedly heard. I wasn't gonna go, but he called me a scaredy Preacher's Kid and dared me—"

"You mean you followed the crowd, huh?"

Daddy laughed to himself as he went back to studying that book again. I was at his mercy. I sat back in my seat and prepared for a long talk.

"Son, you are getting older now, and it's time for you to start thinking about your relationship with the Lord . . . sit up in your seat, boy!"

I did what he asked; even straightened my glasses a little.

"You're my son. You're the son of a pastor, Jeremiah. It's time for you to take your rightful place as a man of God. You listening to me, son?"

"Yes, sir," I responded quickly.

"I hope you are. How many times am I gonna tell you to stop slouching?" He closed the first book that he was reading so hard on. "You know Sister Ruth told me last week that she caught you sleeping during her Sunday School class?"

I couldn't help that Sister Ruth was boring to listen to. She was talking about the creation of God with a room full of kids that had to listen to her tired and drowsy voice. Truth be told, she normally puts half of us to sleep.

"This is more than just you missing curfew a few times or sleeping during Sunday School class, Jeremiah. It's your entire attitude towards the church. It's like you're not interested. Jesus is coming back soon, and you need to be ready. You saved, ain't ya?"

A blank, cautious, yet intrigued look came across my face. I really didn't know how to answer that. I go to church and pray every night and try to do the right thing, but I never asked myself if I was saved.

"I don't know," I finally came to. "I guess I am?"

"Ain't no guessing about it," Daddy snapped. "It's either you are or you ain't. You are either hot or cold. If you're lukewarm, the Lord will spew you out of his mouth."

"I mean, I sometimes pray and go to church and try to do the right thing!" I replied, trying to get my foot out of my mouth.

"That's not enough, son."

"Then what is enough? How do you know if you are saved?"

"You'll know," Daddy answered. "You will surely know. The Bible says in St. John 10:27, 'my sheep heareth my voice.' It's time for you to hear the voice of God, son. It's time to find what you are called to do."

I wanted to say something, but remained quiet. Besides, I didn't know what he was talking about, being sheep hearing his voice. I let out a tremendous sigh to myself as Daddy kept on lecturing me.

"When your brother was your age, he found his calling. He was called to play music for the Lord, like David."

"But I'm not Zeke, Daddy."

"I know that," Daddy said. "But you are somebody too. You are called to do great things, like your brother."

"Why can't I just be like everyone else?"

"Because God called you out. Why won't you accept that?"

"I don't know."

"You don't know, huh?" Daddy said to himself, amazed at my answer.

"Listen to me son, I was eleven once too, and I know the pressures of being a young man growing up. I am your father and I'm looking out for you—not Rodney, not Drew, not even Otis, but you. You're not a baby anymore, son, and right now is the best time to really start building your things on eternal. You hear me, Jeremiah?"

"Yes, sir," I mumbled.

"Good, you can wait for me upstairs in the sanctuary." That was the last thing he said before he went back to studying.

After leaving Daddy's office, I would have rather taken the whipping any day over that talk we just had. I tried to settle myself down, thinking about what God called me to do. I'm not a great singer like Mama or Zeke. I couldn't possibly play any instrument as well and God knows I can't preach to a crowd like Daddy. Maybe this whole calling skipped me. Who am I? Who did God call me to be?

CHAPTER 4

GUESS WHO'S COMING TO DINNER

*D*addy had put me on lockdown after he gave me my licks at home for what I did. I couldn't go anywhere but to church with him all week and had done every chore possible—mowing lawns, cleaning floors, wiping windows, scrubbing bathrooms. It was like being in prison.

Now, I've been writing scriptures down in the living room for an hour. My paper was filled with verses and notes from Proverbs. I listened to the rest of the kids, like Drew and Otis, playing outside. I wondered what they were doing.

Mama came from the kitchen and said, "Jeremiah, I need you to go out to my flower bed and pick those weeds out. We have guests coming over tonight."

"Who are they?" I asked.

"That's none of your concern. Right now, those weeds are your concern."

"Yes, Mama."

"Alright now, make sure you take care of those glasses when you're out there."

Outside, I began trying my best to pull the weeds cluttering up Mama's flower bed. I hated pulling weeds and felt as if time passed slowly when I did it.

"What's goin' on, Jeremiah?" someone called from behind me. I looked back and saw Drew standing outside the gate with a comb in his nappy Afro. I dusted myself off of grass and dirt and met him at the gate.

"I see you been pullin' weeds again, wit' all the holes in ya mama's flower bed."

"Yeah," I replied, still dusting myself off while putting my glasses back on. "Where are you off to?"

Drew started picking his hair, trying to keep it straight. "To the Nelsons'. I'm grabbing me a raspberry soda. Hey, man, wanna come wit' me?"

"I don't know. I'm still on punishment."

"You still on punishment?" Drew asked with some shock. "It's been at least a week now."

I wanted to go with Drew so badly, but I knew I had to ask the warden on duty, which gave me an idea. Instead of *me* asking to go to the Nelsons', I figured if Drew asked, I might get a yes out of Mama since Daddy wasn't around.

"I don't know, Jeremiah," Drew said. "It just seems like that's lying to your mama. I can't do that."

"Drew, it's the only way I can go. It's not lying to her; it's just letting her know that I'm doing a good deed by accompanying you to the Nelsons'."

"I still don't get why I have to be the one to ask. It's *your* mama."

"But you have that Southern-charm personality that Mama loves," I said, trying to boost his ego. "Right now, she would rather hear from you than me."

"OK, OK. I'll ask her for you, but you owe me big time for this one."

"I'll split a Popsicle with you from the ice cream man on my next allowance day, which is next Tuesday," I promised.

"Done!" Drew quickly agreed as he crossed the gate. When he walked up the stairs to knock on the door for Mama, I knew my sentence was getting ready to end early.

***

Later that evening, I was in Zeke's room wrestling with this ugly brown tie I had to put on. Zeke was busy in his own world of music, listening and singing to Rance Allen, coming from his record player.

"I don't understand why I'm wearing these clothes," I complained. "I mean, who are these guests coming over that we have to dress up?"

Zeke turned down his record player and faced me. I guess he was wondering why I was in a complaining mood.

"Ma said she wanted us to look our best, li'l bro," he said. "An old friend of Pop's is coming over, Thomas Helderman."

"Is he an old friend from the church?"

"I don't think he would've been in our church, Jeremiah."

"Oh, he's white!" I scoffed. "You mean we're dressed up and having dinner tonight with whiteys?"

"Jeremiah, where did you get that word from?"

"What word—whitey?" I asked, feeling Zeke's eyes on me in rebuke. "Rodney says it all the time about white people."

"All I know is, you better not let Ma nor Pop hear you say that," Zeke said.

"Aww, Zeke, Rodney's just telling the truth," I said. "What's the difference between us calling them whitey and them calling us what you know what some call us?"

"Whatever you say, Jeremiah. Whatever you say." He turned up his record player, going back into his world of music.

The music may have been more important to Zeke, but I still couldn't believe we were about to have dinner, with actual white people.

When I finally got my tie right, we both heard the doorbell ring. Coming down the stairs with Zeke, we saw outside stood this white man with this boy at his side.

"Walter, it's been so long," the man said gaily as Daddy walked out onto the porch.

"Indeed, it has, Thomas Helderman. How has it been?" Daddy smiled while shaking his hand. "Please, won't you come in?"

My inner thoughts and expressions of disgust must have come to my face because Zeke nudged me and mouthed sharply, "Stop looking like a fool." I took off my glasses and rubbed them intensely as Mr. Helderman and this boy stepped into our house.

"You look good, Walter," Mr. Helderman commented. "Life's been treating you and Carolyn kindly. How long has it been? Seven, eight years?"

"Seven, eight years too long," Daddy noted. "You haven't changed yourself there, Thomas."

"Yeah, just a couple of gray hairs and things." Mr. Helderman chuckled. "Walter and Carolyn, this is my eleven-year-old son, Colton. I used to sometimes bring him by with my wife."

"Wow," Daddy gasped as he eyed the boy with brownish-blond hair and blue eyes. "This is your little one, huh?"

"How are you, Mr. McGill?" The boy politely approached Daddy. "My father has told me so much about you all."

"You've grown up since the last time I saw you, Colton, huh?"

"Who you tellin'?" Colton's dad recounted. "I can hardly keep up with his height and age now. Say, your two boys are growing up, too. This has got to be your oldest right here," Mr. Helderman said, pointing at Zeke.

"How are you this evening, Mr. Helderman?" Zeke asked.

"Thomas, this is my youngest son, Jeremiah," Daddy commented as I greeted him too, slightly.

We all made our way to the living room, and Daddy, Mama, and Zeke sat with the two guests and played catch-up. I sat in a chair closest to the doorway, not wanting any part of this soon-to-be dreadful evening.

"Carolyn, this is some refreshing lemonade," Mr. Helderman said after he sipped from his full-to-the-rim glass of lemonade.

"It's my pleasure," Mama said kindly. "How's the moving process going for you all?"

"It's fine. The sooner the better, though. All my stuff still hasn't arrived from up in Philadelphia."

"And how was living in the big city?"

"It treated me well up there, money-wise. I was doing some assistant baseball coaching at La Salle, but it was long hours. Too much crime, I thought, for a boy to see. Besides, I figured it was time for me to come home and was happy to do so."

"Well, we're glad you're here," Daddy said.

"Walter, I tell Colton here stories all the time about my growing up here," Mr. Helderman replied. "About the times when your grandfather and my father used to do crusades together, spreading the gospel. Those were the good times."

"They sure were," Daddy seconded.

I let out a huge sigh when Mr. Helderman said that. I could already tell where this was going. Grown people just sitting here talking while I'm bored to death—blah, blah, blah, blah, blah.

"Jeremiah, why don't you take Colton here up to your room for a bit while your mother is still setting up dinner," Daddy suggested. I stared blankly back at him as he gave his reason. "Grown adults are talking down here. Besides, you and Colton may have a lot in common, so you two should get to know each other."

Get to know each other? What did me and Colton have in common that we had to know each other? Lord knows I didn't want this boy in my room, my dominion, my privacy, my space. But I sighed and obeyed before I heard Daddy ask, "What does Proverbs 22:6 say?"

I stopped and turned around to face everyone. I took two breaths and recited: "Train Up a Child in the Way it should go, when it gets old, he won't depart from it."

Talk about being ashamed and anxious, fumbling through every word while Daddy nodded, and Mr. Helderman looked amazed.

***

"You all have a nice home here," Colton complimented as he sat in a chair by the wooden writing table in my room.

"Thanks." I was sitting on my bed, continuing to read one of my old Batman comics, trying to make the time go by faster.

"Your mom and dad seem like a pleasant couple," he said, trying to talk to me like we were best friends or something. I gave a light smile and continued reading.

"I see you're reading one of the Batman comics?"

What was this, an interrogation scene or something?

"Yes," I finally replied. "I am reading a Batman comic. Is there a problem with that?"

"No, no," he replied. "Actually, I sometimes read comics too. I like the Superman ones the best."

How long must I be tortured by this boy talking to me? It seemed as if the more I tried to read, the more he talked to me. That's not how the plan was supposed to work.

"So, you from Philly, huh?" There it was. I started my first actual conversation with Colton. I prayed it didn't last too long.

"Born and raised," Colton replied. "Just like you were born and raised here in Cape Creek."

"Yeah, sure," I said somberly, then turned around and asked, "Is your dad always that nice of a person, the way he's behaving down there?"

"Sure, I guess," Colton answered, a bit reserved.

I hastily fired another question. "Even to us black people? Giving my folks the yes-sirs and no-sirs. Enjoying their company. I never see a white man do that before to my parents, unless it's all an act towards us."

"So, is that what you think of all white people?" Colton asked, apologetically.

"I have no problem with them personally. They don't bother me. I just don't like what I see some of them do to black people," I flat-out answered.

Colton nodded his head hesitantly to the truth. "Yeah, I kind of see what you're saying now. But my dad is always nice to everyone he sees. I guess that's his personality." He laughed. "Your mom was really nice to invite us over for dinner."

"Yeah, that's her. Mrs. Florence Nightingale." I sighed. "She even had me dress up for this. Your mom is not here with you all?"

"Not exactly. She died when I was nine years old."

"Oh," I said slowly, saddened. "I didn't know about that."

"It's alright, didn't expect you to know."

A brief pause came as I ran out of things to talk about. I guess he did too since we both stared around the room, saying nothing.

"So, you like being the son of a Pastor?" Colton picked up my Bible with my notes from Proverbs from my desk.

"It's ok, kind of have no choice. I mean, Daddy thinks that our family is a part of this preacher lineage or something. Can you believe he had me recite that whole verse down there, in front of everyone?"

"But you sounded great," Colton assured. "I could tell my father really liked it. Your brother preaches like that, too?"

"No, he's a musical genius at the organ," I said. "My mother is the best singer you would ever hear; my father is a whiz at the Bible and I'm just an eleven-year-old boy who's just in the mix of it all."

We shared a laugh as a small knock came, with Zeke peering through the doorway.

"Colton, Jeremiah, dinner is ready," he announced.

Colton walked out the door behind Zeke, then turned and said, "It's good to meet you, Jeremiah McGill." He stuck out his hand for me to shake it.

I'd never shaken a white person's hand before. If I didn't shake his hand, that would make me wrong, wouldn't it? So, I did what everyone else would. "Sure thing," I replied, shaking his hand in cordiality.

CHAPTER 5

A-B-C AND SCHOOLIN' IS 1-2-3

"**C**ome on, Jeremiah. We gotta get going."

It was the first day of school and Drew came over to my house, fully dressed in his blue-and-white striped button-up shirt, a matching tie, and brown pants. His brown shoes were overly shiny and too big for his feet.

"Drew, it looks like you going to a Holy Ghost tarry service," Zeke cracked. He, along with Mama and Daddy, had a hard time making out what he had on as well.

I sopped up the rest of my pancakes with syrup and went upstairs to finish getting dressed. After brushing my teeth, washing my face, and picking out my afro, I was ready.

Before heading out the door with my school things, Daddy insisted I take my Bible with me. I tried to tell Daddy that this was my sixth-grade year and taking a Bible along with you is just asking for someone to call you a geek. He wasn't budging, forcing me to go back upstairs and grab my bible.

"You look nice today, Jeremiah," Drew commented as we made our way to pick up Otis and Sam.

"Thanks," I said, tugging at the collar of my white shirt. "Zeke was right. You do look like you are going to a church service."

Drew smiled. "Just trying to look my best, since we are the oldest in the school now. What you carrying that Bible for?"

"Cause Daddy told me to," I grunted. "He wants me to read it throughout the day."

"He does?" Drew shook his head. "That's wild."

"I know," I agreed. "This is going to put a dent in my social life, carrying this thing around."

While crossing the street, we saw Otis and Sam standing outside on their porch. Sam looked just as dapper as Drew with his nice button-down shirt distinctly matched with his newly pressed khakis. Otis, who was wearing a solid green collared shirt with pressed blue-jean shorts and tube socks up to his knees, was giving his little brother the rundown.

"OK, Sam," Otis started his pep talk while still straightening up his belt. "You're going to be in first grade this year. Your first time in school. You're a big kid now."

Sam's eyes grew big with excitement, listening to every word his older brother said.

"You have nothing to be nervous about," Otis continued. "You gonna have a good time with Mrs. Riley in first grade. You gonna be learning a lot of new stuff."

"Do I get to paint?" Sam asked innocently.

"Yeah, li'l man. All the time," Otis laughed.

"I can't wait!" Sam exclaimed as he pranced down the stairs, the first headed to school.

J. Skinner Elementary wasn't that far from either of our houses. We were almost there as other kids were either getting dropped off by their parents or just walking along the sidewalk in their best clothes.

After Otis dropped off Sam at his classroom, Drew pointed out Rodney. He was standing with a kid we named Roach, beside the basketball goal of the playground. When he saw us coming, I already knew the first thing he was going to say.

"Look at the preacher kid with his bible," he laughed. "What you gonna do? Quote a scripture for us?"

I clenched my left fist and stared at Rodney without him seeing. I couldn't talk back to him like I wanted to, but my mind took care of it.

"Come on Rodney, leave him alone," Otis said. "Ain't nothing wrong with him bringing a Bible to school."

"Yeah," Roach agreed. "Besides, he can't help it if his daddy is a pastor."

"Aww, I'm just playing with Jeremiah," Rodney said, smiling in my direction. "I'm just glad that we are all in the sixth grade together."

"Me too," Drew said. "Kings of the school."

"That's right, we are, Drew," Rodney confirmed. "And you know what else? I'm gonna make sure I get my own bathroom stall."

"Rodney, your own bathroom stall?"

"Yes, Roach, my own bathroom stall. And if anyone even tries to use my bathroom stall, it's gonna be trouble."

"Not as much trouble as it's going to be having Mrs. Wells this year."

There were two sixth-grade teachers at J.Skinner. One was Mrs. Wells, who had the reputation of being mean and surly and gave out tons of homework, even on the first day of school. Most of my friends were in her class this year, except for me and Otis. We both had Mr. Brian Griffith, the teacher that not one of us heard about. Of course, being Rodney, he already told us that we both were thrown to the wolves, seeing that we may be the only two people of our color in the class.

"Say, say—look, y'all." Drew jumped and pointed his finger slightly over to our left. "Ain't that Christine?"

This girl named Christine that we all knew was standing about four feet to our left with two other girls, talking. She kind of put me in the mind of Mama, with her light pecan skin, and hair tied up into two nicely done ponytails that fell to each side of her face.

"Ooh-wee," Rodney said, with his wolf eyes in Christine's direction. "She knows she lookin' good."

It was no secret that Christine was a lot of the boys' object of affection, including mine. While most boys seemed to ogle and profess their love, I kept my love for the prettiest girl in school locked inside.

"Look, here they come now," warned Roach.

The girls were heading our way. We all stopped what we were saying, trying to play cool. Lord knows we didn't want to make a bad impression already.

"Aye, Christine, come over here right quick," Rodney called, still acting like the wolf he was. If he was putting the moves on her, I hoped it wouldn't work and his plan would blow up in his face.

"What do you want, Rodney?" asked Susie, Christine's unofficial bodyguard, as she and the girls stopped in their tracks to talk to us.

He glanced over Christine's way and asked, "Who's your teacher, Christine?"

Christine looked at the girls she was hanging with.

"Why does it matter to you, Rodney?"

"I'm just wondering."

"Well, y'all see when we get to class."

"Hi, Otis." Sylvia Swain flirtatiously called while waving her fingers to him.

"Hi, Sylvia," Otis replied, unenthused.

Sylvia was wild for Otis. Ever since last year in fifth grade, around Valentine's Day, when she gave Otis this big letter about how she felt. Otis, in return, didn't give her the time of day, which made her even wilder about him.

"Who's your teacher this year, Jeremiah?" Christine asked me politely. My words fumbled right in front of me as I tried my best to remain cool.

"I have Mr. Griffith, Christine," I said in my manly persona.

"You do? Me too!"

My mind was shouting like a Pentecostal preacher on Holy Ghost Sunday. I was really stoked that I'm going to have not only Otis in Mr. Griffith's class but also Christine. Christine for a whole nine months. That hasn't happened since the third grade.

"We girls will see you later at recess," Christine said as she walked off with her friends. "See you in class, Jeremiah. Save me a seat."

"OK!" I replied with glee, waving back at her and smiling like a kid on Christmas morning.

***

Mr. Griffith didn't look like any teacher I'd seen or had before, nor—from what I could already tell—did he act like one. For one, he was just too excited to be there. And for two, he looked too young for anyone to be a teacher, but the girls didn't think so. They were already swooning over his good looks and country-twang voice.

"I hope you all are excited to be here because I'm very excited to teach all of you this year." He rose with a clipboard in his hand, then walked around his desk and sat on the edge of it. "I'm going to call your name in no particular order, and you are going to tell the class something about your family's history."

"What if we can't come up with anything, Mr. Griffith?" someone asked.

"Oh, everyone has history in their families," he responded. "Just think about it. It'll come to you. First up, Mitchell Aiden."

A boy with brown hair at the front of the room stood up and told the class that his father was a chemistry professor at South Missouri

College. That wasn't family history at all, but Mr. Griffith seemed to think it was when he told him it was a good starting example.

As he kept calling each of my new classmates, one talked about how their parents owned certain buildings or properties all around town, and some of them talked about how their parents lived through the Great Depression. Otis talked about his grandfather fighting in World War II and his brother was over there now for Vietnam. Christine shared something we all thought was out of sight. Her great-uncle had been one of the backup trumpet players in Glenn Miller's band back in the twenties.

Otis turned and said, "Hey, who's that kid by the door?"

It couldn't be! In the middle of a boy named Conner speaking, the principal brought in Colton. You've got to be kidding me. Ever since Colton came from Philadelphia to Cape Creek, my life and style had been cramped. This boy came over all the time, and I had to play with him. I had to be polite while I listened to this kid tell me annoying jokes and stories—and now he's in my class?

I prayed Colton didn't have to sit over close to us. I even tried to duck my face under my desk a bit. Sure enough, Mr. Griffith saw an empty desk right beside me and placed him there.

"Jeremiah," he called warmly with those same blue eyes and a wide smile. "How are you doing?"

"You know him, Jeremiah?" Otis asked.

I lightly shook my head no. I didn't want to talk to Colton, especially in front of Christine and Otis.

"Ain't you gonna say something, Jeremiah?" Otis asked, dumbfounded that I wasn't talking. "Introduce us to your friend here."

"This ain't my friend!" I mouthed. I barely even knew the guy. I had to stop myself because if Daddy found out about me not being polite to Colton, my behind was going to be his.

"Colton, these are my friends, Otis and Christine. Otis and Christine, meet Colton Helderman," I said dryly.

"Hello," Colton greeted with a smile as he waved to them.

"Hi, Colton," Christine said. Then she whispered to Otis, "He's kind of cute."

"What's going on, Colton?" Otis replied, shaking Colton's hand. "Nice to have you. I never seen you around here before."

"That's because he just moved back down here from Philadelphia about two weeks ago," I blurted, and Colton nodded. I didn't want Otis to get the idea that me and Colton were best friends.

"Well, welcome to the cool side of the classroom." Otis grinned, and Colton laughed a little. He began to tell him about our first day so far and even the task at hand of us giving speeches about ourselves.

"Well, that should be easy for Jeremiah here," Colton said to Otis and Christine. "Heard him recite a few scriptures myself the first time I met him. He's fantastic."

"Jeremiah, you gonna be a preacher just like your daddy?" Otis asked. "Man, that's square biz."

As I scanned over at Colton, I saw Christine laugh a bit. I was definitely not smiling. I wanted to knock his block off.

"Jeremiah McGill."

Oh, great. It was my turn to speak. I stood up slowly, feeling my palms starting to sweat and feel stiff at the same time. My glasses fogged up and my knees buckled. I knew Mr. Griffith was waiting for me, so I just talked.

"My great-grandfather was known around here as a mighty man of God. He was a preacher who held a lot of revivals around the area. He also founded our church, House of Prayer, Tabernacle of Praise. I guess my dad inherited some of his traits; he's been a pastor for the past eight years."

"That's really interesting. Your great-grandfather passed on a legacy of ministry to your father. That's the essence of history. Excellent, Jeremiah. That wasn't so bad, was it? You have a natural ability in public speaking."

I sat back down as Mr. Griffith finished the roll call. Colton tapped me on the shoulder and smiled really big. I grinned back, then turned to Otis with a look of "Why is this boy bothering me?" on my face as I wiped my palms on my pants.

CHAPTER 6

WHY CAN'T WE BE FRIENDS

I tried to read some of my Bible scriptures during recess today but hanging out with the gang was way more interesting than Noah building an ark. They were all circled up on a grass field by the basketball goals, tossing around a football that Otis brought.

Rodney was doing one of them football stances, trying to look cool. "I can't believe that old bitty, Mrs. Wells," he complained to us. "On the first day of school, and that witch has it out for me."

"Well, it was your fault, Rodney," Roach said. "You know Mrs. Wells don't allow no talking in her class. Although it was funny of you trying to mock her while she was teaching writing."

Rodney wasn't too quick to accept Roach's reasoning. "Still, if big blubber brain Drew over there would've kept his mouth shut and not laughed, I wouldn't have to stay after school for detention."

Drew bowed his head a bit in the humiliation of Rodney's taunt.

"How was y'alls class, Otis?" Roach asked.

"Wasn't too bad so far," Otis answered for us. "Mr. Griffith seems like a cool teacher."

Otis was right. Our morning with Mr. Griffith has been OK. It wasn't a lot of drilling of Math, Reading, and Spelling like it was over at Mrs. Wells. Instead, Mr. Griffith talked a lot about his life down in his home state of Alabama. We also read a lot from our history textbooks, something that was an interest of mine.

"Sounds like you and Jeremiah over here have it easy."

"Yeah, I guess so," Otis agreed. "Mr. Griffith already has Jeremiah reading out passages from our history textbooks."

"You already trying to outshine the rest of us, Jeremiah?" Drew asked, tossing the ball to me.

"Now, you know the preacher's kid here got to be the teacher's pet."

"No, I'm not, Rodney," I argued while attempting to catch the ball. "Mr. Griffith just likes the way I speak. That's all."

"Sure, you're not, sure you're not."

"Say"—Roach looked over at the playground fence—"Who's the white boy coming this way?"

"Oh, Lord. Colton," I shrieked under my breath.

"What's wrong with you, Jeremiah?" Drew wondered.

"Nothing, Drew." I prayed Colton would bypass us for the sake of peace and tranquility. I knew Rodney wouldn't be too thrilled to see someone like Colton, but as soon as Otis called him over, it was a dangerous move on his part.

"Otis, you know this cat?" Rodney asked, eyeing the fresh meat up and down.

"Yeah," Otis replied. "Y'all, this is Colton Helderman, Jeremiah's friend. He's in our class this year."

Everyone turned and looked at me in shock, and I stared agape at Otis.

"What's going on, Colton? My name's Drew." He gave him one of his special high-five tricks, which Colton didn't get, of course. No one got Drew's special high-five tricks. "Any friend of Jeremiah's is alright with me."

Next to be introduced was Roach.

"Your real name's Roach?" Colton asked.

"Well, it's Rowen, really, but everyone here calls me Roach," he explained.

By the time Otis introduced Colton to Rodney, the atmosphere shifted. All this time Rodney hadn't said a word. If looks could kill, Colton would've been dead and buried by then. Instead of shaking Colton's hand, he nodded his head slightly and said coldly, "Nice to know you."

"Say, Colton, we were going to play a little tackle football before you came," Otis said. "With you, we have even numbers."

"Yeah, since you're gonna be hanging with us, this is a good way for you to learn the ropes," Drew added.

"OK, sure," agreed Colton.

While the rest agreed to some football action before going back to class, Rodney stayed frozen in position, tossing the football up in the air and eyeing Colton like a lion stalking his prey.

"Come on, Rodney, don't you want to play with us?" Roach asked.

"I don't know, Roach," Rodney said. "I don't know if Colton here can handle a little contact from us."

"What's that supposed to mean, Rodney?" Otis said.

"Come on, Otis, you know that Colton here don't want to play football with us," Rodney said.

"I don't know why not," Otis disputed. "We are all boys. Colton here's a boy. He can play just like we can."

"What I mean is, Colton doesn't belong here. He ain't one of us."

"Aww, Rodney, we're just playing a game of football," Roach said. "It's not like we're asking for a blood sample."

"Hey, I didn't make the rules. I just follow them. He should be with his kind, and we should be with our kind," Rodney said, sticking to his principles.

"Now, Rodney." Otis's voice got really stern and deep. "You have no right to say that. Colton is cool people, and cool people don't always have to be our kind."

"If y'all want me to play, I'm not playing with whitey over there."

"It's my football, and I say Colton plays. We all want to play. What's your excuse?"

"You all want to play, huh? Why don't you ask Jeremiah here if he wants to play football with Colton."

"Jeremiah ain't gonna care about Colton playing football with us, aren't you, Jeremiah?"

"Huh?" I didn't know what to answer as Otis looked at me with his faith lying in my hands. If I said Colton could play with us, then I would be lying to myself because truth be told, I really didn't want him to. It was nothing against him, but all this hanging out was too much. He sat by me in class, talked to Otis and me the whole time during lunch, embarrassed me when he said I was good at reciting scriptures, and now wanted to play football with us. I needed some sort of break from him.

"I . . . I . . ." I began. "I . . . uh . . ."

"Come on, Jeremiah," Otis said. "Don't be like Rodney. You are not like Rodney. This is your friend, remember?"

"See, Jeremiah over here knows what's up," Rodney boasted. "As I said, white boys should play with their own kind, just like we do."

"Rodney, you disgust me. You would rather sacrifice—"

"You know what, Otis, it's OK," Colton spoke up. "I shouldn't get my new clothes dirty, anyway. Maybe next time. I'll see you all in class."

"See, told you Casper, the Friendly Ghost, didn't want to play," Rodney said.

Watching Colton flash that winning smile as he walked over to the playground burned Otis to the core. His silence spoke for miles about how he was feeling, and it wasn't good. I thought Rodney was about to get it, but I was wrong.

"Sometimes you just shock me, Jeremiah," was the last thing Otis said before dropping the football and walking off.

"What did I do that was wrong?" I questioned.

"Aww, you didn't do anything wrong, Jeremiah," Rodney said as he walked over to pick up the dead football. "In fact, you did the right thing by sticking up against that Colton kid. We didn't want him over here in the first place."

With all that was said, I expected Rodney to get the blame. "I said nothing, though, Rodney. I didn't say that Colton couldn't play—you did."

"Hey Jeremiah, it's all good," Rodney said, throwing his shoulder around me. "I knew you didn't want to make anyone mad, because you tried to do the Christian thing and all, but I knew what you were thinking. We all did."

I thrust his arm off me but couldn't answer fast enough before the teacher told us all to line up. I walked over to my class line, feeling jumbled in my brain. Rodney did all the talking. Rodney was the one who said Colton couldn't play because he was white. He said coloreds should stay with coloreds and whites should stay with whites. I didn't say anything close to that. Why was I getting the blame by Otis?

CHAPTER 7

FORGIVENESS WITH A SLICE OF HUMBLE PIE

*I*t had been a whole week since Colton really talked to me since what happened at recess on the first day of school. Rodney still swore up and down that I did nothing wrong. At first, I was OK with it, thinking Colton was going to come around and we would talk again. Now I wasn't so sure.

That Monday morning, while writing, I tried to have a casual conversation with Colton. I even told him some scriptures I'd been reading. Do you know what he did? He just nodded his head and went back to work. I thought maybe he would respond better during recess or lunch when we could talk. No avail. That's when this sense of content turned slowly into a sense of unshakable guilt.

"How you think you did on that science test Mr. Griffth gave us?" I asked Otis.

We were walking home from school with Sam at his side when I decided to pick at his brain. I was going to bait him along until I found some lead way with me and Colton.

"I think I got at least a B. Why you ask?"

"No reason," I replied, thinking of another angle. "You and Colton talk to each other a lot in class. Does he talk about, you know, me and if he's mad at me or anything?"

"Oh, I know where this is going," Otis said. He escorted Sam to their porch and told him to wait by the door for him. "You want to see why Colton stopped talking to you."

"You noticed, huh?"

"Who wouldn't notice?"

"Well, do you know if Colton's mad at me or anything?" I asked, pressing the issue.

"Man, I can't tell you what me and Colton talk about. It's all sorts of stuff." He walked up the steps to his house, taking out his key to let his little brother in, then turned to me and said, "If you feel that he's mad at you, why don't you try to talk to him?"

"I did," I answered. "I tried to talk to him all day during school. He just seems unresponsive."

"You let him down, Jeremiah. You hurt his feelings."

"I still don't know how. I wasn't like Rodney, calling him names and such."

I stood still on the sidewalk, waiting for any more fragments he could give me.

"All I can say is this, Jeremiah. You're not like Rodney or the rest of them. You have a heart, and whatever your heart is telling you, follow it. I'll see you tomorrow."

Even though it was small, I took in what Otis had to say before going inside—*follow my heart.* My heart led me to my house phone that night to try calling Colton to clear my conscience. I was going to talk to him and tell him everything and that it wasn't my fault, but he wasn't available to come to the phone.

By Thursday, I had to seek counsel and found it in the Great and Wonderful Ezekiel. I hoped paying him fifty cents for five minutes would do me some good. I poured out my heart to Zeke in the living room as he played the piano.

"I just didn't know what to do," I told Zeke. "I mean, I didn't mean to make anyone mad."

Zeke finished playing and went into deep concentration for three seconds. He looked over at me and asked, "Do you know anything about Mr. Helderman, Jeremiah? Why does he like our father so much?"

"Huh?" I thought. "What does this have to do with Colton?"

"You on something, li'l bro. Mr. Helderman's family has always treated Pop's family with the utmost respect. They never looked at us as colored or black people, but saw us as equals. You know Mr. Helderman's father was a minister around here? That's how they've gotten to know Pop's family."

"I don't need no history lecture," I responded. "I need some advice on how to get this thing smoothed over."

"OK, OK. So, you say Otis invited Colton over to play football with you all, right?"

"Yeah," I answered.

"And you said that everyone but Rodney wanted to play, correct?"

"Yeah."

"Then, when Otis asked you, you didn't say yes, or no. Am I right?"

"Yes, that's the whole story. What should I do?" I begged.

"Well . . ." Zeke pondered for about another five seconds and answered. "You are just going to have to face the fact that you are just as much to blame as Rodney."

"What?" I exclaimed. "What are you talking about?"

"Think about it, li'l bro. Rodney obviously doesn't like Colton because he's white, and when Otis asked you about the same thing, him playing football with you all, you were in the middle. You didn't say no, and you didn't say yes. So, that makes you just as much at fault."

I thought about it. I actually sat there and thought about it, and you know what? Zeke was right. It was my fault Colton's feelings got hurt. I didn't stick up for him. I was wrong for what I did.

"Then what should I do?" I asked.

"You are just going to have to be nicer and more considerate of Colton. You remember the first time he and Mr. Helderman came over? I could tell that whole evening that you didn't like Colton."

"You didn't have to take him to your room and basically be his conversation piece that whole evening."

"You were upset about that night because Mr. Helderman and his son were white, and you had to show kindness to them."

"I guess you're right," I confessed.

"See, that's the first step. It's like what the Bible says. 'Treat others the way you want to be treated.'"

"Who are you supposed to be, my advisor?"

"Hey, you paid me for my help. I'm just doing my job."

"OK, fine, I'll do it," I agreed. "What's the first thing I should tell Colton?"

"You are gonna have to tell him tomorrow morning that . . ." He stopped and faced the piano once more and said, "I'm sorry, but your time is up," in a monotone voice.

"What?" I cried. "That wasn't five minutes, and you know it."

"Please give the great and powerful Zeke fifty more cents for more counsel."

"But I don't have any more money to give you," I confessed, pleading for more time for counsel.

"Well, you better ask for an advance on your allowance from Pop, 'cause this service doesn't operate without cash money," Zeke said as he went back to playing his stupid songs.

Then came Friday. As the month of September inched away, the heat and humidity came back with a vengeance. It was hotter than in mid-July, with us having to pay the price. Our air conditioners busted down by 8:30 that morning. By 9:00 a.m. we were all sweltering out of our clothes. You could surely hear our moans and groans, including mine.

"Class," Mr. Griffith began as he stood up. "I know it's too hot to do anything work-related today. So, we're going to have what we call news time."

"What's news time, Mr. Griffith?" one of the kids named Layton asked from the far left.

"I'm glad you asked, Layton. News time is when we catch up on the latest news stories and share them with a close neighbor."

Understanding what he was talking about so far, we all nodded.

"You are going to grab a newspaper from the back, pick anywhere you want and just read the paper."

When he told us to go, we all walked slowly to the back of the class and grabbed newspapers wrinkling up from the heat. I took my paper and sat in a corner by myself.

I wasn't a big fan of the news or stories. Any time I got a paper, I read the comic section. I read the Peanuts comic to myself. Lucy accused Charlie Brown of being a blockhead for making fun of his friend Linus. I sure felt like Charlie Brown right now, a blockhead for what I'd done. I looked over at Colton sharing with Otis what was probably something from the sports section.

"What you reading, Jeremiah?" a familiar voice asked with a smile. Christine. Now normally, I would be smitten right then as she looked at me with those brown eyes. She looked so pretty that day, with her hair pressed back so nicely past her back.

"Oh, nothing," I replied, bogged down with other thoughts. "Just Charlie Brown."

"Charlie Brown? You're such a big fan of comics." She laughed.

"Yeah, I feel like a blockhead like he is right now," I disclosed.

"Blockhead? Why you feel like a blockhead?" she asked.

I wasn't going to tell her. I really wasn't, but in that moment of desperation, I kind of had no choice.

"Christine, can I ask you something?"

"Sure," she replied, sitting down beside me.

"Christine, I got this problem with a friend of mine. What do you do when you talk to someone and then all of a sudden, he stops talking to you? We weren't the best of friends, but I still miss this person being around me. I don't know if he hates me or not. It's just this feeling I have."

"What did you do to make this person hate you, Jeremiah?"

"See, that's the thing. I messed up and I don't know how to fix it. I tried everything—talking to him, explaining myself, I even gave him space to come around—and nothing seems to work."

"Well, have you ever tried to say sorry to this person?"

"Say sorry? I couldn't do that."

"Why not?"

"Because that will make me look like a wimp."

"Well, I know if someone did something wrong to me, I would want to hear sorry and know they mean it. Just put your pride aside and tell him how you feel."

"May I have your attention, please?"

The class was in a tight hush when Mr. Burns came over the intercom. There were normally only three reasons our principal addressed us over the class speakers—to do the morning announcements, the parting announcements, or to call someone down to the office. We all braced ourselves for the worst.

"Students, teachers, and staff, because of the situation of our air conditioners, we are dismissing school at ten thirty."

The tight hush quickly turned into thrilling chaos. This was like a kid's dream come true—getting out of school legally. We didn't even bother to hear the rest of the announcements until Mr. Griffith called us back into decorum.

"Once again, we are dismissing school at ten thirty. Thank you," our principal signed off.

"Oh my gosh, Mr. Griffith, what are we going to do?" a girl named Ashley sitting close to the door asked frantically.

"Boys and girls, put your newspapers back by the window ledge, grab your stuff, and have a seat at your desks."

We all did as he said, putting our papers away and heading to our desks with our belongings in our hands. While we sat there watching the clock tick slowly, Mr. Griffith quickly passed out homework and papers to sign. I guess he wanted to get out as much as we all did. I looked over at Colton, who was putting his things away and grabbing papers from Mr. Griffith. It was now or never, my last chance to talk to him before the weekend.

"So, you're reading the latest issue of Superman, huh?" I asked, smiling like he did when we first met.

He looked at me with a strange, surprised look on his face and finally answered. "Yeah, I haven't finished it yet, but it looks like it's pretty interesting."

"Really? What's it about?"

"Well, it's about Superman's pal Jimmy Olsen. He's a smart guy who is a master of disguise and . . ."

He stopped, having caught on to what I was doing. He packed up his comic and headed for the door to line up, leaving me standing there. That's when I had to lay it all on the line. I took Christine's advice and followed behind him and gave him the apology of the century.

"Listen, Colton, I'm sorry for what I did back at recess on the first day of school. I was wrong, and I didn't mean to hurt your feelings. I know I shouldn't have acted the way I did, and I can't take it back. We don't have to be the best of friends; I just don't want you to hate me."

Now, the waiting game. No words came as the 10:30 bell for dismissal rang. Instead, in that split second, as he was walking out of the classroom, Colton flashed his winning smile slightly and said, "See you later, Jeremiah."

CHAPTER 8

SUPERMAN VS. LEX LUTHOR

*O*tis and Rodney almost got into a fight after school. I should've known it was coming, the two powers colliding for dominance.

"We've been standing out here for ten minutes already," Rodney nagged. "What's taking that Otis so long?"

"Give him time, Rodney. When I talked to him, he said he's bringing someone with him and Sam," Roach informed.

Otis even had me curious about who he was bringing. Our answer didn't delay any longer as Drew spotted him out with Sam on his shoulders and the mystery person. When Rodney looked and saw who it was, you could see that smile literally turned upside down.

"Jeremiah, I know Otis ain't bringing him to play with us."

He expected me to answer that? I knew no more than the rest of us did as we watched Colton coming our way.

"Uh, I guess he is," I answered.

Boy, did the cuss words come out of Rodney's mouth for real with no one to stop him. If Otis thought Rodney was going to allow Colton to play with us, he better look out for the fireworks coming from Rodney's mouth. Thankfully, as Otis set Sam down, Roach intercepted them just in time with his own conversation.

"You brought Sam, my man, out here today, huh, Otis?" Roach asked playfully.

Sam smiled at his partner in crime. "Hi, Roach."

Roach reached over toward Sam and gave him a trick hand motion. "I see that you've been practicing our secret handshake."

"Yup, I have," Sam said. "Got any candy?"

"Now, you know I got some candy," Roach answered as he reached into his back pocket and pulled out two pieces of bubble gum and a Banana Split Chew.

Sam ripped open a piece of bubble gum so fast and almost popped it into his mouth before Otis stopped him.

"Sam, what do you say to Roach?"

"Thank you," the grateful six-year-old said.

"Alright," Otis laughed. "Now you go over there and play by the playground. I'll come over there with you in a little bit."

Sam was excited to go over by himself to that big playground. It was like a jungle adventure in his eyes.

After everyone said their hellos, we couldn't help but notice this cold look coming across Rodney as he looked at us, then at Otis, and finally at Colton, who was still flashing that famous smile. I braced myself as round two of Rodney's mouth started to play.

"Look what Otis brought to the field, y'all. Casper the Friendly Ghost."

Laughter from Roach and Drew exploded as Rodney began making fun of Colton. The more laughs Rodney received; the more jokes came flying out of his mouth.

"Come on, Rodney, enough with the jokes," Otis finally said in defense. "Colton came for the same reason we all did—to hang out."

"Well, he should have thought about that before he came out here. Fly away, Casper. Go back to where you came from."

Otis was getting more agitated with each joke, balling up his fists trying to hold everything inside and resist striking the Jokester.

"Aww, chill, Otis, you know this is how we get down. If he can't take the heat, he can take his white self out of the kitchen."

I felt bad for Colton. The way Rodney was treating him was wrong. I thought Colton was going to cry and cave into Rodney, but something else happened. Colton stood his ground. He wasn't scared of Rodney or his jokes. He was laughing right along with them, and suddenly had the comeback of the century.

"That's good, really good jokes, but I say talk is cheap from a guy that throws the football like a sissy girl at recess."

Oh, did that quiet him down. Talking about Rodney's skills was fighting words, literally. It got so quiet; I stopped feeling bad for Colton and started feeling scared for his life. Rodney marched up to the brave soldier, Colton, who wasn't backing down for nothing.

"You trying to knock on me, white boy?" Rodney asked.

"Just stating the obvious things," Colton replied without missing a beat. "You clown on me; I clown on you back."

"Looks like you came to play a man's game, huh?"

Colton stepped up closer to him like a challenge. My heart beat faster and faster. "You can say it like that. Where I'm from, we call people like you punks."

Oh, did I chuckle at that, for Rodney was taken aback. No one had ever stepped up to the so-called bad boy in this manner, but Roach beat me to the punch.

"You gonna let that city white boy talk down on you like that, Rodney?"

"Ain't nobody scared of Colton," Rodney answered. "We're just gonna let the game of football do the talking. Me and Otis are going to be the captains."

Go figure.

We all lined up like the army in the middle of the field, and the two quarterbacks picked their platoon. In the end, though, it was Rodney with Drew and Roach on his team against Otis, me, and Colton. Rodney looked over at Otis's team and spotted Colton out.

"You just bought yourself a whoopin', Colton," Rodney vowed.

With two hard snaps from his finger and a signal, all of Rodney's team seemed to have vanished from our sight.

After Otis had his minute of going over what we had to do, I pulled Colton to the side. "Do you know what you've just done?"

"What do you mean, what have I done?" he responded calmly. "I'm not scared of Rodney."

"I'm not scared of him, either. You don't have to be—just be smart," I said. "He's out for your blood."

"Jeremiah, Otis was right about you. You're so funny." He chuckled. "I appreciate you worrying for me, though—but don't worry. I faced kids like him all the time back in Philadelphia. Had to fight a couple of them, too."

Colton's bravery floored me. All the things I tried to tell him and presage him about. The end result was him just laughing in joy. We rejoined Otis until I saw Christine walking up to us with Susie.

"Hey Jeremiah," she said with that beautiful smile.

"Hi, Christine. What y'all doing out here?"

"We just walked around; saw y'all down here so we came to say hi. I see that you are with Colton here."

I then told her all that happened between Rodney and Colton and how it led to this impromptu game of football. Colton's bravery towards Rodney impressed them both.

When she saw some of her friends down the street, Christine waved toward me. "See you later, Jeremiah."

"We better get back too, Jeremiah," Colton reminded me. I was so entangled by her beauty and her talking to me that I didn't hear Otis calling for us.

We were clustered on the other side by the trash cans as Otis gave out his plays and assignments. It was determined that Otis would be the quarterback, Colton was his center, and me playing a lineman.

"First team that makes three touchdowns are the winners," Rodney established. "Past the two trash cans is our field goal, while past the drinking fountain is yours. Got it?"

We all assumed the huddle position and our quarterback called the first play: 42 Jackie. He says he names his plays by famous athletes he likes.

"Forty-two Jackie," Otis broadcast as we positioned ourselves for the first play.

"Forty-two Jackie, hike!" Colton spiked the ball back to our fearless quarterback. Otis threw a perfect spiral to his open man, Colton. He caught it and took off, running a little deep down the field until POP! Drew got to him midfield with a tackle that opened the game's challenge with cheering and banter from Rodney.

The next drive came from Rodney's team. Roach spiked the ball back to Rodney, who then maneuvered his way around me and Colton and threw the ball straight to Roach. Roach thought he had the touchdown made until Otis took him down. As the two got up, Otis gave his usual words of encouragement to a disheartened Roach.

"Nice drive, Roach." Otis stuck out his hand for a sportsmanship shake.

Roach halfheartedly shook it. "Yeah, thanks."

"Jim Brown thirty-two," our quarterback announced. "Jim Brown thirty-two. Hut, hut, hike." Otis quickly found a way out of Rodney's and Drew's blocks and took off with the speed of lightning. Our football hero weaved his way around and around his opponents. It was a sight to see. No one could stop him. He passed Roach and ran all the way down past the water fountain for a touchdown. The score was now one touchdown for us on Otis's team and nothing for Rodney's team.

Rodney had to score a goal quickly and knew just the person to do it. He passed the ball to Drew, the biggest and tallest person on the team. Otis, Colton, and I tried to take him down, but instead, he gave us a ride all the way past the two trash cans.

"Touchdown!" Rodney screamed with excitement as they rushed over to celebrate. The score was now tied one to one.

We couldn't drive the ball to the end zone during the next play, which led Rodney and his team to get the ball back. That's when Rodney's overconfidence began to show. He tried one of his whacked-out plays in which Drew and Roach would switch positions and Roach would basically run the ball. Somehow in the shuffle, Roach forgot the play. Drew couldn't get the ball fast enough as Colton dived over, caught it, and ran all the way for a touchdown.

Rodney shook his head in frustration and anger. "Drew, where were you on that last drive?"

"I'm sorry, Rodney. I didn't mean to mess up."

"Of course you didn't. Your blubber brain got in the way. Now they up two to our one because of you."

"Hey, ease up on Drew there, Rodney. It's just a friendly game," Colton said, handing him the ball.

"Who asked you, Casper? You know that touchdown was lucky."

"All I'm saying is, let's just play the game."

"Alright, we'll play."

I didn't like the way Rodney said that, nor the sneer on his face while taking the ball. It looked like he was formulating a plan to get back at us. I knew I was right when he pulled Roach to the side and whispered something deep and Roach responded, "Oooh, Rodney, that play's gonna get 'em."

I attempted to warn my team, but it was too late. Otis was calling the next play.

"Sixty-seven Ali, sixty-seven Ali, hut, hut, hike."

The heat was on Otis. He got Colton's attention and threw the prettiest spiral his way. He took off like a cheetah in the wild. Colton was hot on the trail for a touchdown, gaining speed by the minute. I started cheering for him as he passed Drew and Roach. He made it shy, almost to the end zone, tasting victory against Rodney's team until POP! Rodney snuck in from the side of Colton and took him down hard. That tackle was so hard, so vicious, and so dirty. It stopped the entire game.

"I told you not to mess with me, Colton. I'm the king around here," Rodney boasted. Colton sat up, shaking the loose grass off his hair, and dusting his shorts. As I reached out my hand to help him up off the ground, Rodney was still spitting his fireworks.

"This is my house, you hear me? My house."

"Leave him alone, Rodney," said Otis. "You tackled him and that was enough."

"Yeah, Rodney, let's just finish the game," Roach suggested.

No matter to Rodney. He didn't want to finish the game and was still in the moment of his glory when Drew and Roach came over.

"I told you, Otis, ain't no white boy gonna run me. You let your friend get tackled by the lion over here. What does that say about you, you whitey?"

In a split second, Otis pushed Rodney to the ground. We all gasped. He dived over at his target and pinned him to the ground. Then Otis lifted Rodney by the collar of his shirt and waited for Rodney to talk so he could strike him down for the count.

"Go ahead, Otis, hit me," Rodney enticed. "You know you want to. Defend him like the Uncle Tom you are."

I thought Otis was going to beat Rodney's brains out when he said that. The sounds of encouragement for a fight got louder and more intense. It would have been like Superman versus Lex Luthor. Of course, as Otis looked around at us, then at Sam on the playground, Otis's superstrength returned to normal. His mind wanted to fight Rodney, but his heart wouldn't allow it.

"Aww, come on, Otis, you ain't gonna steal on him?" a letdown Roach wondered.

Otis stepped back, threw Rodney on the ground, hollered "Let's go" at Sam, and walked off. Rodney spat out blood as Otis walked away. Roach went over and picked up the football and started heading home.

"Hey, where you going with that football, Roach?" Rodney asked. "We can still play the game."

Roach turned and answered, "Otis left, Rodney; the game is over."

CHAPTER 9

DOWN AT THE POTATO PATCH WITH DADDY AND MEMORIES OF UNCLE CLARK

Autumn was here at Cape Creek. The leaves were blowing off the trees in their pretty yellow, brown, and orange colors. The weather was changing from the blaring heat of summer into a crisp tint of nice, cool air, which in return made everyone seem a little nicer. I was even friendlier to Colton, and he became OK in my book.

The season of fall also meant the harvesting of sweet potatoes. This was the first year I went along with Daddy and Zeke to collect potatoes. They drafted me around six o'clock to be their extra hands. We loaded up in an old pickup truck and traveled up the road for a couple of hours to the countryside a little past St. Louis.

For the longest time down in the field, me and Zeke put more effort into our work than conversation. My brother and I knew that Daddy didn't want a half-done job on the harvest of sweet potatoes.

"Be sure to place your potatoes in the buckets with ease, Ezekiel," Daddy cautioned, coming down Zeke's row.

"Aww, don't worry, Pop, I'm not going to mess them up," Ezekiel said. "I've been picking potatoes with you since I was Jeremiah's age."

Then Daddy crept over to my side. I felt his eyes scanning inside my bucket as a light "Hmmm" came out of his mouth. "Looks like your side's coming along alright, Jeremiah."

"It is?"

He smiled. "Yes, I think it is. Keep up the good work."

For this being my first time, I enjoyed working with Daddy in the field so far. It wasn't much of anything, but it was one of the rare times I got to see my father as a human being. He wasn't this big pastor or important figure I had to mimic or look up to. He was simply Daddy.

"Boys . . ."

Me and Zeke looked at one another, knowing Daddy was about to get started.

"All of this picking reminds me of when me and Clark was young and had to work with my mother, chopping cotton on this land down past Sikeston. You talk about hard work—that lady would put us to work from the crack of dawn Monday through Saturday."

"Monday through Saturday? That's almost every day."

"It was every day, Jeremiah. We worked till our fingers were numb. We had to make sure the cotton was right. If there was one slight mess-up, we didn't get paid. I had a lot of fun back in those days."

"Fun? How?" I wondered.

"Yeah, Pop, I have to agree with li'l bro. Who wants to spend their childhood working all the time?"

"It was a good life, Ezekiel; you can believe that. A life with a slower pace," Daddy said. "We didn't have all that y'all have now. We lived in a one-room shack with no running water. Even had an outhouse."

I had read about outhouses in one of my textbooks from school. They were these small, framed buildings with a deep toilet inside. From what I'd seen, I never wanted to use one of those.

"I don't see how you survived back then."

"We lived, Jeremiah. That's what we did. I remember on Sunday mornings at my grandfather's church with Mama. Hearing him preach with such power and sing such conviction."

"Daddy, is it true what they said about Elder Johansson?" I asked. "Was he as strict as everyone says? Did he put people out of the church that didn't live right?"

Me and Zeke heard Daddy laugh. "Grandpa Johansson believed in living holy, breathing holy, and being holy," he answered. "I guess he did put people out that didn't live up to that standard."

"That seems kind of hard, don't you think, Pop?"

"Maybe so, Ezekiel, but Grandpa Johansson lived what he preached. In fact, he was the reason I wanted to be a preacher. I knew I could speak in front of people and scriptures came easy for me to memorize and recite. I even used to have church outside on your great-grandpa's shack with all the neighborhood kids as members."

I laughed along with Zeke. Daddy was still smiling, still sharing more details of his past life.

"Every Saturday morning. I used to be preaching, whooping, and hollering like no other," he continued. "They cried and cried, saying 'Lord save us' and everything while I pretended to lay hands on them."

Daddy began singing some of them old hymns he claimed were classics, like "Swing Low, Sweet Chariot" and "Down By the Riverside." He really got into it and started clapping his hands and stomping his feet.

"I used to do the preaching and your Uncle Clark used to do the singing and playing of his harmonica. You talk about having church every Saturday morning — that's how our family was and still is. We are special and anointed."

"Pop, why do you think Uncle Clark left the church and never really came back?" Zeke asked.

I barely knew Uncle Clark since he died before I was born. We heard stories about him, not much, though, especially since he was well known for being a famous blues singer down in Memphis. Even back then, when Zeke asked Daddy about it, he had little to say. However, just seeing our uncle's picture on his record, Missouri Blues, Zeke admired him even more.

"Your Uncle Clark was a good man, Ezekiel," Daddy said, gathering up his memories. "He was determined, bold, strong-willed, and that boy could sing anything. He and that harmonica of his—he used to always make beautiful music."

Daddy lowered his eyes.

"When he left the area at seventeen, I knew it was the biggest mistake in his life. He was determined to make something of himself and that harmonica."

"I guess that was when he made that record we found upstairs, in Memphis?"

He nodded his head again. "He recorded a few of them. It brought a lot of buzz down in Memphis and gained plenty of attention for him to travel around the country, but the fact still remained about your uncle—he belonged in the church."

He paused, as if he was wondering if he should continue.

"You know, I remember the last time me and your mother saw Clark. He had come home from the road and stayed with us. Clark had no money left and was broken on the inside. Papa Johansson gave up on him and Earla Mae was too sick to take care of him. His soul was tired and needed to come back to the Lord. We all loved Clark and tried to lead him down the right path of God. We tried to get him to come back to God, just like the Prodigal Son. He just needed somebody to believe that he could change. Sadly, that never happened."

Daddy breathed in deeply. "When he passed, that hurt me so much. That was my youngest and only brother, and I felt when Clark died, a piece of me left as well."

"You can't blame that on yourself, Pop," Zeke then said, trying to comfort our father. "You did what you could do. I bet you Uncle Clark understands that."

"One day, you boys are going to have to make your own decisions about your lives and your lives with the Lord. You both are almost getting to that age, and you're not always going to have us around."

"Oh, Daddy, don't say that."

"I know you don't understand it, Jeremiah, but as you grow up, there's a lot of temptation out in the world today. A lot more than what me and your mother grew up with. It can be easy for a young man like you or your brother to get caught up in something he has no business being in. It can be easy for you two to be led astray. Lord knows what me or your mother would do if we found out you guys were in real big trouble."

"Aww, Pop, me and Jeremiah's going to be alright. We have more sense than you think we do," Zeke said. "Besides, I'll make sure to keep Jeremiah in line if necessary."

"Well, I know you're good at that," Daddy said before we all laughed.

After filling the last buckets with potatoes, it was time to use all of our strength to haul them heavy suckers over to the truck. When we finished, we had about twenty-five big buckets of potatoes sitting by the back. Then he pulled the keys to the truck out of his pocket and tossed them to Zeke, signaling that he was going to practice driving us home like he had been the past couple of weeks.

"You boys can start putting these buckets carefully on the back of the truck while I gather everything else from the field."

I nodded and Zeke gave his usual "Everything is everything" spiel. I could tell when he said that, he wasn't going to work right to the minute like I was going to. He was retreating into his own world of music again, singing slightly to a tune from Gene Martin.

I looked back over to where Daddy was towards the field. His talking about his childhood really had me thinking. Everyone else in the family knew where they fit in except me. Lord knows I don't want to disappoint Daddy or the family legacy, but I still don't know what I'm anointed or special at.

CHAPTER 10

WHEN KENNY COMES MARCHING HOME

That evening, Mama was in the kitchen putting the finishing touches on her first sweet potato pie. It smelled so good. I went over closer to her, hoping she would give me a little taste.

"Don't touch that pie, Jeremiah," Mama warned as she set it on the kitchen table. "It's for after dinner."

Mama turned down the stove where the chicken was boiling. I helped her by washing the silverware. She was humming an old spiritual, which was lovely to hear.

Finally, she struck up a conversation. "I heard you all had a great time picking this morning with your father."

I nodded my head, telling her all about the stories Daddy shared about his childhood and his times with Uncle Clark.

"I tell you, your father may be a genuine man of the cloth, but he can be funny when he wants to be." She went back to humming that lovely hymn, adding some words to it about asking the Lord to touch her in the spirit, then her mind, then her soul. I got out of the way as she came over to the sink to drain the boiled potatoes.

"Mama, how do you sing so good?" I asked.

"Well, I really can't answer that Jeremiah," she answered. "Like I always tell people, my gift comes from the Lord."

"Did you know you could sing when you were little, like around my age?"

"I really never thought about it," she said. "When I used to sing with my family, people would stop and listen to us. They used to be blessed by our music. I never knew I was called to sing for the Lord. That didn't come till later."

"Boy, I wish I knew what I was good at doing," I said. "Seems like everyone knows their gifts and calling in this family but me."

Mama slowed down her stirring. "What about your writing?" she asked. "Your teacher told me that he really enjoys reading your work, as well as everyone else."

"Yeah, I guess that's true," I answered. Mr. Griffith has been giving me the best marks in class on every essay I've written. He says I had a natural talent for putting words together.

"Don't worry about it so much, Jeremiah," Mama added. "Whatever God has for you; he will reveal it to you in due time."

At that moment, a friendly knock came on the door. Mama answered to let themselves in.

"That must be Deacon Wallace with the greens from Helen," she said to herself. "Come on into the kitchen," she then announced.

Who came into the kitchen wasn't Deacon Wallace or his wife, Helen. It was Otis with some man beside him. He looked a little older than Zeke, dressed up in a green army uniform, shiny black shoes, and a beret stationed perfectly on top of his head. He looked familiar, too familiar. I couldn't make out who he was at first, but when he nodded toward us and smiled heavily like Otis, it hit me. He wasn't a stranger at all; he was Kenneth Wilson, and he was home from Vietnam.

Mama looked up and saw the wide smile from the young soldier. She cupped her hands over her face, trying to contain her excitement.

"Kenneth Wilson?" Mama called, stunned like I was.

Kenny walked over to Mama, arms out for a hug. "How you doing, Mrs. McGill?"

"I'm fine. How have you been, son?" asked Mama, still smiling.

"I'm doing the same," Kenny responded.

The two embraced for around maybe fifteen to twenty seconds. There was no containing any emotions anymore—Mama was almost in tears. She held Kenny out like he was her own son, shaking her head in disbelief, crying more tears. At last, gathered up her words. "When did you get here?"

"I've been in Cape Creek since late last night. I landed in Mississippi around a week ago, where I took the Greyhound all the way up north to Memphis, then caught a ride from one of my buddies who headed up north to St. Louis. I didn't tell anyone I was back in the States because I wanted to surprise Mama."

"I know it thrilled Judith to the moon when she saw you home," said Mama. "I bet you she almost fainted, didn't she?"

"She didn't faint, but I think I almost gave her a heart attack. She screamed so loud, I think some of the neighbors almost called the police thinking I was a robber or something. Little Sam instantly ran to me. Otis over here was scared to hug me, like I was a ghost or something."

"You didn't recognize your own brother, Otis?"

To this, Otis just nodded with a tiny bit of laughter. He was still standing in the background, away from the kitchen door.

"Aww, Otis, she was just messing with you," Kenny said. "I promise you he hasn't said two words since I've been home. He acted like he didn't want to come with me to see y'all."

"He's just taking it all in, Kenny. The boy hasn't seen you in almost three years. I bet you're glad your brother's home though, aren't you, Otis?"

"Yes, ma'am." Otis grinned at us.

***

The next day at church, Daddy made a special point to announce to the entire congregation that Kenny was home from the war. You can see the excited looks on the people's faces when they saw the soldier sitting with his family. Even after the service was over, many people were welcoming him home, asking all sorts of questions about his time in Vietnam.

"I'm sure glad Kenny's back home," Drew said. We were standing over a grass field beside the church.

"Me too," Roach said. "He looked mighty spiffy in his uniform. How did he look up close when you saw him, Jeremiah?"

"He looked like himself to me," I replied. "Except with a mustache and a slight beard."

"Say, Rodney, aren't you glad that Kenny came home?"

Rodney ran his long finger through his hair and shrugged a bit. "Don't matter to me none," he replied. "My daddy said he shouldn't have never gone over there to fight in the first place, in a white man's war."

"What choice did he have, Rodney?" I asked. "Kenny was drafted, and he couldn't say no to that."

"Maybe so, Jeremiah. I still say he should've been like Muhammad Ali and went to jail instead."

We were all taken aback by Rodney's response and attitude as he walked over to where some of the teenagers were by the side of the church.

Before the evening service, I was busy catching up on my homework Mr. Griffith assigned when Kenny found himself back over at our house. This time, he was sitting outside on our porch with Daddy, Deacon Wallace, and another man named Deacon Freeland. After finishing solving division equations, Mama said I could go out and sit while the men talked until it was time to go.

"Say, young buck, ain't nobody messed with you while you were in the army, did they?" Mr. Wallace asked playfully.

"Not at all, Mr. Wallace. I know how to take care of myself," Kenny replied, laughing a bit. "If anyone tries to mess with me, I'll just give them that one-two knockout punch like you taught me when I was thirteen."

"I hope you continue to come to church, Kenny," said Deacon Freeland. "You know Walter was going to ordain you to be a youth minister of the church. That was before you left for the war."

"You still remember that, Pastor?"

"Of course," Daddy said. "You were one of the best students I ever had. Sharp as a whip with the Word and knew more passages than even some of the preachers. Ministry was your calling, and still is."

"Honestly, I don't know if I remember those scriptures from long ago or not," Kenny admitted. "I haven't really read the Bible in over three years."

"That's alright, son, as long as you still got God inside of you."

"Kenny, did you stop by and see Laura?" Mama asked, changing the subject swiftly when she stepped out. "I know I'd seen her around here somewhere since she has been home from her schooling up north. She would be happy to see you."

"I stopped by their house and talked to her a bit," he revealed. "Didn't really say much to her but hi."

"Well, you should stop by later on tonight, take her out to eat, and catch up with her. I know you two have a lot to talk about," said Mama. "Still thinking about marrying her like you did when you were in high school?"

Look at Mama, already planning a spring wedding.

Kenny shrugged his shoulders and chuckled a bit. "We'll see about that, Mrs. McGill."

"I still say you two should do it. The sooner, the better. I can't see anyone else loving her more than you would."

It was good to see Kenny back home where he belonged. That contagious personality that could turn your sadness into gladness, your frown right side up to a smile, and your tears into laughter was coming back out a bit. Him joking around with everyone, trading stories, and laughing it up.

There was a slight moment of silence before Deacon Freeland asked, "So, Kenny, let me ask you. How was it really over in Vietnam?"

Kenny sat back for a bit, figuring how he was going to answer as you could tell his mood shifted. It was as if he didn't want to talk about it. "Honestly, Mr. Freeland, just like I told everyone, I can't talk about that right now. It's a lot for me to even think about it. I just thank God I'm home and pray I will never have to go back."

"You'll have plenty of time to tell your story, Kenny," Daddy replied. "Just know that you did your country a service. You should be proud of yourself."

"Yeah, I guess I should, huh, Pastor?" Kenny said, still a bit uneasy.

The room went quiet, yielding to what was just spoken. Me and Ezekiel stared at each other. With only the sound of Mama's record player oozing out the sounds of Shirley Caesar from the kitchen, Deacon Wallace spoke up.

"Believe me, son, I know how you're feeling right now," he said. "Seeing you in that uniform reminds me of my days when I was around your age, in 1942, fighting over in France during the big World War Two. I was eighteen at the time, a kid myself, and I'd seen the same action you've seen. You just remember that I know, young buck, I know."

Kenny stayed quiet as Deacon Wallace kept speaking.

"I lost too, lost a lot of friends from the big war. You're talking about a kid who didn't even want to fight, but I had to. My country depended on it. I was called and I answered it, just like you and many other men had to."

Mama sighed deeply. "Lord knows we've been fighting long enough over there. I just don't understand why we are still there."

"No one knows, Carolyn."

"Well, President Nixon made a promise to end the war, and we have yet to see that, Pastor," Deacon Wallace said. "Let's face it, he's just another man that thinks he has a plan and don't."

"Carl, don't you think you're stretching it a bit?" asked Deacon Freeland

"Well, it's the truth. Look at them, sending our young brothers and sisters out there in the jungle but on a wing and a prayer. And yet we have our own wars here at home. People can't find jobs, homelessness in the streets, racism, and violence everywhere."

Deacon Wallace finished and not one of us responded. Kenny stood, signaling that he had to get home for the evening.

Mama stood as well, saying she had to get back to finishing up her cleaning. "Kenny, it's good to see you home," she said, and everyone nodded. "Thank the good Lord above you made it home."

CHAPTER 11

LOVE SICKNESS AND GREAT AND WONDERFUL EZEKIEL CURE

"Alright, which one of y'all gonna play against the king himself in a game of four square?" Rodney asked. He was going for the record of the most wins in a single month's game.

"I'm in," Roach said, coming in behind Drew. "Just as long as I get the first dibs on a square."

Colton, Otis, and myself also agreed to play. Everything was going great today until Rodney dropped the bombshell of the century in the middle of his turn.

"I plan on asking Christine to be my girlfriend after school today."

I almost choked on a loogie caught down my throat. My ears had to be deceiving me because Rodney couldn't ask Christine out—he just couldn't. What if she said yes to his jive-talking ways? It wouldn't be right, for him going out with the girl I liked.

"I don't know, Rodney," began Colton, throwing his opinion in. "From what I know of Christine, I just don't see you two together."

"Shows how much you know, Casper," mocked Rodney. "For your information, Christine got the hots for me. Y'all haven't noticed her checking me? She's been giving me the look."

Rodney put his lips together and made kissing noises.

"I'm sure I've seen that look before. On a fish at my house," Drew laughed.

We all looked out and saw Christine playing double dutch with her friends. Her beauty still dazed me. How I wished I could get her to even notice that I liked her for more than just a friend. How I wished I had the confidence to just tell her how I felt, everything that had been in me for so long.

"Ooo-wee, looks like someone besides Rodney has a little crush on Christine. Ain't that right, Jeremiah?"

"Huh?"

I must have been daydreaming about me and Christine a bit too hard. How was I gonna get myself out of this one? The last thing I needed was my secret crush on Christine Hill to be revealed.

"I saw you, smiling so big," Roach said.

"No, I wasn't," I claimed, lying through my teeth. "I wasn't smiling like that."

"Aww, don't try to sugarcoat it now, Jeremiah. You like Christine Hill, don't you?"

"Jeremiah likes Christine Hill? That'll be the day when pigs learn to fly," Rodney said.

"How would you know, Rodney?" asked Otis. "Christine's an attractive girl, Jeremiah's a nice guy, and from what I see, I think Christine kind of digs you too, Jeremiah."

"She does?" I raised up so I could hear the rest of what Otis had to say. He basically sealed the deal in my mind. It didn't matter who agreed, even though they slowly did after thinking about it for a bit.

"You hear this, Rodney?" Roach just couldn't let it go, trying to start something. "Otis said that Jeremiah and Christine should be together."

"It'll be like the geek with the chic," Rodney said as he swiped the ball from him. "I mean, why would a stone-cold fox like Christine go out with someone like Jeremiah?"

"Don't listen to him, Jeremiah," Colton told me. "You're far from a geek."

"Yeah, Jeremiah, you're not a geek," Rodney started. "You're a square whose daddy's a pastor and who loves comic books. He's nothing like his older brother, Zeke, whose at least popular. Zeke's cool, hip, and slick with his rap. You're just a plain ole' preacher's kid with owl glasses and nappy hair."

Rodney and Roach laughed, and I felt myself becoming embarrassed, like a hermit crab.

"Hey Jeremiah, no need to get upset. I'm just messing with you. You're tight with us. Besides, you said you don't like Christine anyway. There's no need to lose your cool."

***

There had to be something that could make me look a little cool to the girls. How could I make them see that I'm not just this plain ole' preacher's kid? Maybe if I had one of them mustaches like Rodney claimed to have, I could gain some attention. I took one of my black crayons and created a mustache in the bathroom. Hey, it did make me look a lot older and cooler. Looked almost a little handsome from a squinting angle.

"Jeremiah, what are you doing in the bathroom?"

The shock of Zeke opening the door made me lose focus on my shading.

"Don't you ever knock anymore?" I asked while hurrying to put away the black crayon. "What if I was taking care of some real business?"

"I knew you weren't taking care of no real business, Jeremiah," Zeke replied. "I'm going down to the Nelsons."

"So, what does that have to do with me?"

Zeke said that he wanted me to grab my jacket and come with him. I did what he said, not in the mood to fight. I headed out of the bathroom, pretending nothing happened until Zeke looked at my face all funny.

"What you got on above your lips?"

Good grief! In all my rushing trying to cover everything up I forgot to take off the mustache. I grabbed a piece of tissue and smudged it off my face.

"So, how was your day today?" Zeke asked as we walked to the store.

"It was OK," I replied, keeping my guard up. I returned the favor by asking how his day was. He answered it was great and started singing. I had to give it to my brother. He was incredibly good-looking and popular. I wished I had the perfect smooth skin, wavy Afro hair, a stunning smile, and talent like no other.

When we made it to the Nelsons', I followed Zeke over to the aisle where the men's personal needs were. He was looking at the cologne section.

"What in the world are you looking at cologne for?" I asked him. "I'm sure Daddy has some you can borrow."

"Pop doesn't have this kind, Jeremiah," he answered.

I watched as Zeke searched attentively through each shelf, high and low, for this specific cologne he had to have. I knew he finally found it when his eyes met up with this green box of cologne named Brut. He picked it up as well as some minty-fresh toothpaste, some smelling-good deodorant, and dental floss.

As Mr. Nelson rang up Zeke's items, he turned to me and asked, "You want to get us some candy, Jeremiah—my treat?"

"Uh, sure!" I finally answered.

"Why don't you grab us three 100 Grands, since they're your favorite."

I set the three 100 Grands alongside Zeke's stuff. I collected the two bags, one with Zeke's stuff and the candy and the other with Mama's meat, and we headed back home.

"Hand me one of them candy bars, Jeremiah."

Zeke hurried and opened that candy bar up and started chomping down, expecting me to do the same.

"Everything cool with you, Jeremiah?"

"What do you mean?"

"I'm just saying, ever since you came home from school, you haven't been yourself," he observed. "You even didn't eat one of those candy bars."

"Well, I'm fine."

"I know this sounds crazy, but if you have a problem, you can always talk to me. I am your big brother and probably went through the same things you're going through."

"I said I'm fine, Zeke."

"Alright, Jeremiah, don't be so uptight. Forget I asked."

We walked about two more feet down Mound Street. I couldn't let the opportunity pass. I turned to my big brother and asked, "Zeke, why do people call me a preacher's kid?"

Zeke paused his walk and looked back at me. He probably never thought I would ask that sort of question, to him at least.

"What do you mean, li'l bro?" he wondered. "Whose calling you a preacher's kid?"

The last person I thought I would be talking to about my troubles was my own big brother, but who knows? Maybe he had the secret I needed to be and look cooler.

"Zeke, if I tell you something, you promise you won't laugh?"

"I'll try not to," he swore.

"I'm serious, Zeke. You can't laugh, and if I tell you, this time you ain't gonna charge me any money for your help like you always do."

"OK, Jeremiah, I won't."

"And you gotta promise me that you won't tell Mama, Daddy, or any of them friends of yours."

"Fine, Jeremiah, this will be between you and me. Now, what's going on with you?"

Alright, here it goes.

"Well, there's this girl I really like at school, and Otis tells me that she may like me back, but I'm afraid she may go for someone hipper than me."

"Well, who's the girl?" he inquired.

"I don't know if you remember her, but her name is Christine Hill."

"Christine Hill—the one we used to live by?"

"Uh-huh," I confirmed with a thick smile on my face. It happened every time I thought of her. "Well, Rodney likes her a lot too and when he found out I liked her, he called me a preacher's kid."

"What's wrong with being a preacher's kid?" Zeke asked.

"Zeke, a preacher's kid isn't going to get me anywhere in life. I need something bigger than that. I got to have an edge like Rodney or a cool look and popularity like Otis."

"Why do you want to be like Rodney or Otis for, Jeremiah?" Zeke asked. "All you have to do is just be yourself."

"Don't you get it, Zeke? We are sons of a pastor who spends most of our week either at home or at the house of the Lord. Besides, you're lucky to have people that notice you. You don't wear glasses or have to put on these dorky-looking clothes. Rodney's right, Christine ain't never gonna like someone like me, a preacher's kid."

The conversation went to a pause for a moment from my admission. I was looking for a joke from Zeke to cheer me up, but he looked at me and said, "Jeremiah, did I ever tell you that you have what those superheroes you read about all the time have—a superpower?"

"What are you talking about now, Zeke?"

"I'm talking about your power that is bigger and cooler. Something that Otis, Drew, Roach, and Rodney all wished they would have."

"Oh yeah, what?" I was all ears.

"Jeremiah, we have special and secret powers called the Holy Spirit."

"The Holy Spirit?"

"Shoot yeah, little bro, the Holy Spirit," he began explaining. "How do you think Pop can preach the way he does? Ma says all the time she can't sing without it. I had my experience when I was ten and it changed me. Before it, I was dorky and all, just like you."

"You were?"

"Yeah, I was. You were too young, but you don't think I went through the same thing you're going through right now? I've been called all kinds of names growing up."

"They called you names, Zeke?"

"Of course," Zeke said. "They called me church boy, holy roller, square. Basically, everything Rodney calls you. When the Holy Spirit came on me, none of it mattered. I developed confidence in my gift of music."

"But I'm not like that, Zeke. I can't sing like Mama, and I sure don't know scriptures like Daddy. I still don't even know what I'm called to do."

"Sure you do, Jeremiah," said Zeke. "You remember when you were about six years old and did Easter Speeches with the kids? You basically preached the Lord's Prayer."

While my big brother had a fond memory of my performance, I barely remembered it. The only part I had a memory of was seeing Mama crying her eyes out and Daddy standing up taller than the Empire State Building. It was like a big deal to them.

"You received a standing ovation when he was done," Zeke nudged me a little on my shoulder, filled with pride. "Sure, a lot of people could've done it, but the way you did it was so unique. It was like you transformed into Superman from Clark Kent."

"Ha, ha, ha, very funny," I responded.

"Don't worry, Jeremiah, I'm not laughing at you. I'm laughing because I see myself in you. You just don't know how great you are. You may not see it, but everybody else does."

"They do?"

"Sure they do. Just like Pop says, we are different and anointed. Just like what Mr. Griffith says about your papers and the power of your words. People love it. Do you know how many papers I'd wish I got an A on? I was terrible at writing and it's natural for you."

I smiled a bit at Zeke's compliment towards me.

"See, I told you had a superpower, and you didn't even know it. You're a smart kid, li'l bro. You just need the Holy Spirit to bring it out of you again."

As I stood back and watched my older brother smile at me, I was proud to call him the Great and Wonderful Ezekiel McGill. He just didn't know how much better he made me feel as I followed him home and devoured my share of the 100 Grands.

CHAPTER 12

A CHRISTMAS MIRACLE

As October turned into November, and November quickly went to December, I was in search of the Holy Spirit. I didn't know what it was going to take, but I was determined to get it, just like Zeke did. I've been asking every Sunday in church for the Lord to fill me with his Holy Spirit. It took a minute of me not getting anything, but eventually, it happened, on the evening of Christmas.

It was a silent night, a holy night, in that everything around Cape Creek was calm and still. I was in the bathroom straightening my tie in the mirror, humming to "Amazing Grace," one of the songs Mama normally sang every Sunday. I didn't know why I was humming, let alone thinking about service. It was like I was happy to be going to church, which was a rare thing for me.

Zeke rushed me out of the bathroom, saying that it was time to go. Since finally receiving his license, my big brother had been volunteering himself to drive us everywhere, which also meant that we had to be on time. I promise you; he was worse than Daddy when it came to being punctual.

On the way to church, I was enjoying Mama and Daddy, listening to them talk, until I looked outside. There was a blue misty cloud following us. I just sat there and looked at it. I didn't even bother to tell anybody. I figured no one would believe me, as I was its lone witness. At every corner Zeke turned, there it was. At every stop sign, it stopped right along with us. I swallowed my lump of fear as Zeke whipped the long Stallion around the church.

There was barely any room inside the church. It seemed that everyone in the town was here. Zeke had to push through the crowd just to get to the organ. Luckily, I found Drew and sat right beside him in the back row.

"Good thing you came when y'all did, Jeremiah, because I didn't know how long I was going to hold this seat for you," he told me.

"They still coming in?"

Drew nodded. "Since we first opened the doors around thirty minutes ago."

I was looking at the people still coming in as Zeke began playing music on the organ.

"Looks like service is getting ready to start."

The choir was really singing that night before Daddy came forth. They sing well every week, but that night something was different. Every song they sang had the whole congregation stirred up, playing their tambourines, stomping their feet, and shouting hallelujah and amen. Hardly anyone was sitting down, and the melodies seemed to come down from heaven itself.

After Mama and the choir sang down the house with songs of praise, Pastor Walter McGill, my father, came with the word of the Lord. He was in top rare form, coming out of the book of Exodus with the familiar story of Moses and the children of Israel crossing the Red Sea. He was at the part where God told Moses to stretch forth his rod in faith and the sea parted. After telling how they walked across dry land towards their promised land, Daddy talked about how the people went into a celebration. I would usually be unmoved by the preaching by now and had even been known to fall asleep in the back with Drew, but that night I loved it. My old man preached with authority and power, and I was all into it. It mesmerized me, watching my daddy like he was a total stranger.

"As we leave the year 1971, and enter into another year of 1972, God said that the enemies you see today, you shall see no more after this day!" Daddy proclaimed to the saints at the top of his lungs from behind the pulpit.

That's when Zeke fired up that organ, and Mama was up in the choir stand leading songs of victory with the choir backing her up, and the whole church went into this crazy praise service.

"Come on and praise him, children!" Daddy sang. "Praise him for your victory because the Lord made your enemies your footstool!"

My father was feeling the Spirit himself. He came from behind the pulpit and walked up and down the pews, laying hands on people. Some were being filled with the Holy Ghost, others were being healed, and some were just praising the Lord. The church was rocking. In the center of the aisle, so many people were dancing, speaking in tongues, and crying out to God.

There must've been another twenty to thirty minutes of praising God before the benediction finally came. Daddy signaled Zeke to break on the organ, got back on the pulpit, and addressed the people.

"I hear the voice of the Lord saying someone here wants to rededicate their life to God. Let's do so now. Come down now, please."

A few people around the church came from behind the pews and walked down to the front, where the ministers lined up and were ready to pray.

"I hear the Lord saying that someone wants to give their life to Christ. Today is your day. Come down now."

The second time Daddy made the call, I looked up and more people were at the altar, giving their lives to Christ.

"Jeremiah, look at all these people getting saved," Drew said.

Drew was right. I looked up again and indeed it was fifteen men and women lined up down there with their hands lifted and eyes welling up with tears. I'd never really paid any attention to this part of the service before, but the whole church seemed to be at a standstill along with me as Daddy reached over and prayed for each person down at the altar. They showed so much emotion and humility; it made Mama and a few other saints that knew them to break down and cry, knowing that their prayers were finally being answered. I was happy for them too, even though I didn't know most of them. Everyone around me applauded, thanking Jesus that a lot of the saints were coming back to God. Daddy hugged and greeted each one, but he wasn't finished.

He got back up on the pulpit and announced, "I hear God saying that if you don't have the Holy Ghost, right now is the time to get it."

Most of us sat there, looking around to see who was going down when Daddy made the call again.

"You going up there, Jeremiah?" Drew asked. The way he asked me was like I should be going down there or something.

"I don't know." I scooted to the edge of his seat and faced the aisle, watching the few people that were finally going down to the altar. "I do want the Holy Ghost, but I don't want to be down there by myself."

"Well, if you want it, go down there," Drew recommended.

After a few more seconds of contemplating as more people went down, I looked over at Drew and made up my mind. "I'm going down there."

I stood up, making my way over to the center aisle and down to the altar. I wasn't the only one in our crowd that was down there. A few others had their hands lifted at Daddy's instruction.

"Yes, that's it, young people. Come on down, come on down to the altar. God wants to fill you with his power," Daddy said.

Suddenly, what started as a few people down at the altar turned into a big crowd. Daddy then told everyone at the front to start crying out to God like never before and told the saints standing around them to just pray. At first, it didn't look like anything was happening, but Daddy must've felt something, because he said, "That's it, keep crying out. Don't hold nothing back."

One by one, I heard people begin speaking and bucking in the Holy Ghost, but not me.

"That's it, that's it right there. You got it, you got it!" Daddy said with excitement to each one.

My eyes were closed, with me praying to God to fill me with his Holy Spirit. Still, nothing is happening. I opened my eyes to look at who all were shouting and praising. Over by the wall, my eyes suddenly jumped. I swear unto you, the same blue mist that had followed us earlier, the same blue misty cloud that had surrounded us, was making its way inside the building. I looked around to see if anyone else was seeing what I was seeing. The cloud was traveling all around the front of the altar, and everyone that it passed started speaking in tongues.

"Come now, come now if you don't have the Holy Ghost," Daddy cried with urgency. "Come now while the water is being troubled. The Glory of the Lord is here. Don't wait any longer."

I kept praying and crying, praying, and crying until something hit me like a jolt of electricity. I felt a change in my tongue.

"Thank you, Jesus," I heard myself say. "Hallelujah, THANK YOU, JESUS! HALLELUJAH! THANK YOU, LORD!"

My stomach bubbled over with the power overtaking my body. My feet felt like they were on fire, and I danced all over the place. I felt a warm sensation up and down my spine. I screamed and hollered and cried, snot running out off my nose. I didn't know whether or not anyone was looking at me, but by this time, I really didn't care.

"HALLELUJAH! HALLELUJAH! HALLELUJAH!" I cried, then heard myself speaking in tongues. The sounds were flowing out of me, like what happens when Daddy prays. I kept speaking and crying, speaking and crying, crying and speaking until I had no more strength left.

When I came to, my eyes shot open. My clothes were torn up, I felt my glasses leaning over to the left a bit, and I even had to find my right shoe, which was over by the drums. I remember going back to my seat as Deacon Wallace got up and said the last words of the evening.

After service was dismissed, you wouldn't believe how many people came up to Daddy just to say that they loved the message today. With everyone that spoke to him, hugged him, and complimented him, one would think that Daddy became a man that was more than human. He just thanked each one and said his usual words of him being a humble servant of God. Sister Ruth and Mother Pearl were one of the last ones to talk to mama and daddy that evening. They both were still in awe of the presence of the Lord that swept over the building.

"When I tell you the Glory of the Lord came into the church tonight, it sure did. Had a good time too, didn't we y'all?"

"Yes, we did Sister Ruth," agreed Mama.

"And to see that many young people get saved and filled with the holy ghost, that was so beautiful," Sis Ruth commented.

I didn't say a word, trying to figure out what happened to me. Everything around me looked different. It was this bright and new feeling, like what the old folks said about being born again. My hands looked new; my feet looked new too. Even on the way home, I was quiet. It wasn't until we reached the front yard of our house that Mama noticed my abnormal silence.

"Jeremiah, are you alright?" she asked.

"Oh, yeah, I'm alright Mama," I quickly answered.

"Are you sure? Because you haven't said anything since we left."

"I'm fine Mama."

With Mama not pressing anymore, she and Zeke got out of the car and headed into the house. I was still in the car, contemplating whether I wanted to ask Daddy all about what happened back at the church. He was drained and needed some time alone as I too got out of the Blue Stallion and headed into the house for the evening.

"Daddy?"

"Yes, Jeremiah."

"Nothing."

"Daddy."

"Yes, Jeremiah."

"Nothing, no wait Daddy."

"What is it, Jeremiah?"

"Never mind."

"You sure?"

"Yeah, I'm sure."

There wasn't anything that needed to be said. He knew, just as I knew, what happened tonight. I finally received it, what everyone was talking about, what the old saints would tarry for, what Zeke told me and what Daddy prayed about. I received the Holy Ghost.

CHAPTER 13

JEREMIAH'S FIGURING

*I*t was a Sunday morning in the middle of January. I was downstairs ready to go to church when I found Daddy sitting in the living room. He was going over his Sunday message, thumbing through his Bible, and writing on his notepad on the coffee table. The aroma of black coffee was warm and inviting, leading me to join him.

"Is there something you want, Jeremiah?" he asked, without taking his eyes off the page.

"No, sir," I said. "Just thought I'd join you while we wait on everyone else."

He motioned me to come in and have a seat beside him. I really didn't have any particular reason, but I just wanted to be with my old man. Ever since the Christmas service and all that he did, I had major respect for my father. I understood him and his life more than before. As I sat there and watched him work intensely, my mind was so full of questions that I couldn't help but ask.

"Daddy, how long does it take you to prepare for a message on Sundays?"

"It depends," Daddy responded, still reading the Bible. "Sometimes it can take a day or two, but if God is really pressing, some messages can take up to weeks at a time. Why do you ask?"

"No reason," I said. "I just always wanted to know."

I sat there for a few more seconds, listening to him hum beautiful melodies of hymns and praises while writing down scripture from the book of Ephesians. He stopped writing and finally looked at me. His eyes bucked out of his glasses with shock. "Well, look at you, wearing a tie for a change."

I had decided to put on my brown tie, which matched the brown trousers Mama got me for Christmas. I must say, it did fit me nicely.

"Aww, come on, Daddy, I wear a shirt and tie every Sunday," I said, trying to play it off.

"Yeah, when we force you to," he replied. "You look very handsome, son, more like a young man than a boy." He then went back to preparing, but not for long before he asked, "You ready to talk about what happened?"

"Talk about what?"

"I mean, about you getting filled with the Holy Ghost. You've been kind of quiet on it lately."

"Oh, I didn't know I was supposed to talk about it."

"I'm not asking you to," Daddy said. He sat up and faced me again. "I just wanted to make sure you understood what happened to you."

"Yes, sir, I kind of understand—maybe not as much as you all do, but I understand a little."

"That's good. Being filled with the Holy Ghost is nothing to be scared of or ashamed of, Jeremiah. It's just a part of your knowledge of God."

"Yes, sir." I could've ended it right there and said no more as Daddy went back to reading and humming, but I didn't. "Daddy," I went on, "there was a blue-misty-cloud thing in the church. It followed us all the way from home to the church."

"You must be talking about God's Spirit."

"You saw it too?"

"Of course I did. I saw it when it came into the building and hung over the people. I saw it when it was over you, too."

"When God touched me, it was like something burning inside of me. I was dancing and shouting all over the place. I was going crazy and screaming at the top of my lungs."

"That's part of the Holy Ghost, son," Daddy said, laughing. "It's just like what the prophet you're named after said in the Bible—fire shooting up in your bones. And I must say, seeing you being filled with the Holy Ghost for the first time was quite entertaining for me and your mother."

"Oh, I didn't mean for all that, but I just couldn't help it."

"I know you couldn't, Jeremiah. We all went through it. Ezekiel was filled with the Holy Ghost when he was around ten years old, and he danced just like you. The Holy Spirit filled me when I was about nine years old, and let me tell you something, I was scared out of my mind."

"You were?" I gasped, surprised at Daddy's admission of fear.

"Yes, I was. I took off around the church hollering like someone was attacking me. I didn't know what to do with it, Jeremiah. I had no idea what having the Holy Spirit was all about."

"I wasn't scared when I was being filled, Daddy."

"I'm glad you weren't," Daddy said. "I'm also glad that God answered my prayers. I prayed that the Holy Spirit would fill you that night, Jeremiah, and that God would use you in a mighty way."

"Yes, sir," I said humbly. "So, what happens now? Since I have the Holy Ghost and all?"

"Change," Daddy said. "Your life is going to change drastically because now you have power. You hear the old folks say that you won't walk or talk the same. You'll have a new way of thinking and a new attitude—that's what's going to happen to you if it hasn't begun yet. I also prayed that God would show you who you really are in him."

"How will I know that?"

"Just keep reading his Word. Keep seeking God. The more you read God's Word, the more you'll understand it and who you are in him. You are somebody great—you just have to believe it."

***

Mr. Helderman kept his promise to attend one of our morning services. There he was, sitting with his son, Colton, in the back of the church. I have never seen so many saints looking at our visitors. Most of us hadn't been to a white church before, nor had we seen how white people behaved in such settings. Judging by what we'd seen on them Catholic shows, they were more reserved when it came to praising the Lord, but not Mr. Helderman. He gave more hallelujahs and amens than some of the saints who had been there for years. You could tell that he was really having a good time.

Daddy was busy talking with Mr. Helderman after service, and I waited with Colton in the office area. He walked around, admiring all the books and church artifacts like he was in a museum. Like every new person that comes to the church, he was staring at the picture of Grandpa Johansson.

"I really like your church, Jeremiah," he said, smiling at me. "I'm sorry if my dad is acting a little strange."

"What for?" I asked.

"For all the times he shouted out during service and bragged about your father to everyone. I know it was kind of embarrassing."

"No, it's OK," I said. "That's how people are when they hear my dad preach. He just gets them all excited."

"He really does," Colton agreed. "I can see where you get your writing and speaking skills from."

"Thanks," I said. "I've been really thinking about what I'm supposed to do on this earth, my calling and everything. Seeing my dad preaching lately kind of sparked something in me. Like maybe that's what I want to do in my life."

"That's great Jeremiah," Colton said. "I can see you doing that, like another young Martin Luther King Jr."

"Aww, you're just saying that because my dad's a Pastor."

"But it's more than just that, Jeremiah."

"It is? How so?"

"I don't know, but you're different. You're not like the rest of the people I've come to know. You're special. Whenever you speak in front of us and Mr. Griffith or sing during music class or anything, it's different."

You know, Colton's faith in me shocked me. He really believed that I can be like my father. As we said our goodbyes until school time tomorrow, I heard the others coming in behind. They all looked intrigued.

"Are you alright, Jeremiah?" Drew asked.

"Yeah, why do you ask?" I responded.

"Because you were talking to Colton. You've never talked to Colton before. You sure you're not sick?"

"Drew, I'm fine," I assured him. "We were talking about how much he loved church today."

"Aww, come on, Jeremiah, we all know you better than that," said Roach. "Don't tell me that you're getting ready to kick the bucket on us and trying to make up with everyone."

"Jeremiah ain't dying on us, Roach," said Otis. "He's just trying to be nice to him. That's the right thing to do."

"Oh brother," Rodney huffed. "First Otis and now Jeremiah being an Uncle Tom to Colton. Well, I'm not going to be getting close to Casper, the Friendly Ghost."

"Now, you know what the Bible says, Rodney. It says that we have to love everyone, even those who have a different skin color," Drew said.

"Besides, Colton may be an alright person when you get to know him. I've come to like him as a friend."

It was shocking to hear those words coming out of my own mouth. Even though Colton and I had been spending more time together the past few months, more than I had with any other white person I'd met before, I'd still considered Colton to be just an acquaintance. That all had changed. With all his corny jokes, his winning smile, and his big heart, we had grown to be more than just acquaintances. I realized we had grown to be friends.

Rodney was still shaking his head in disbelief. "It'll be a cold day in hell before I turn nice and be friends with him," he laughed. Sister Ruth then announced to us kids that it was time for us to come inside of the cold weather.

CHAPTER 14

EVERYTHING AND EVERYONE CHANGES

As the cold winds and snow of January began to melt away, February seemed to fly by, and before we knew it, we were headed into the middle of March. Kids around the neighborhood were playing outside again, and neighbors were planting and tending their gardens. Jack Frost was slowly letting up his cold winter grip on the town of Cape Creek.

I usually would have been outside enjoying the nice spring days like the rest of the kids. Instead, I'd been finding myself reading—not the latest Batman comics, but the Bible. It was like what Daddy said to me. The more I learned about God, the more I began to understand and like it. I was even paying more attention to the sermons in church and reciting more scriptures in Sunday school for Sister Ruth, more than any other kid in there.

One day as the other kids were playing at recess, I sat alone on the bench, reading the letter to the Ephesians, until I heard someone say, "Man, Jeremiah, you've been reading your Bible a lot lately, haven't you?"

I looked up and saw Otis smiling really wide like he always did. He said he had been watching me read for the past minute or so without me even noticing. He sat beside me and peered over my shoulder.

"What verse are you studying this time?" he asked.

I showed him the letter to the Ephesians. The church was told to stand against the devil in the sixth chapter. I explained to him that we, as the soldiers of the Lord, must have the full armor of God in order to defeat Satan and his devices. Otis looked like a few of the church members looked when Daddy preached—kind of getting it, but still out of the loop.

"Man, I don't know how you can understand all of that in one chapter," he said. "I can barely get through one verse of the Bible without getting cross-eyed."

"Well, it was kind of that way for me too," I said. "At first it seemed like a foreign language, but after a while it all kind of made sense."

Otis chuckled. "I guess there is hope for me, since a son of a pastor had to learn, too?"

I laughed with him, yet wondered why he was still here. I thought he would've left by then and joined the rest of the gang.

"How come you're not playing basketball?" I asked.

"I came to see you. Haven't talked to you in a while," he answered. "You don't hang out with us anymore like you used to, Jeremiah. It's like you disappeared."

He was right. I did do a disappearing act. I'd been so caught up in getting to know God that I kind of gave up going on some of Rodney's latest adventures and quests, something I'd thought I would never do. It kind of made me feel bad, and out of place with my Bible in my hand.

"Hey, man, no need to feel sorry," Otis said. "Shoot, we may need you one day preaching the good news. You know Rodney needs the good Lord to check him from time to time."

"Amen to that."

I put my Bible away and gave Otis my full attention. After we talked about how hard the new math in class was, he told me he was signing up for baseball with the Capaha Arrowheads. They were the rich team of the town, with most of their young players coming from families of doctors, lawyers, and other important people as such. Otis obviously didn't come from an affluent background. In fact, the only reason Otis was playing on the Capaha Arrowheads was because Colton's dad was one of the coaches that year, and he had personally asked if Otis would play with his son, and Otis had happily agreed.

"How has Kenny been?" I then asked. "I didn't see him at service the other day."

Otis stared at the ground for a couple of seconds before looking up to answer. "He's doing alright. I guess."

Since returning to school from Christmas break, Otis seemed more serious and worried than before, and no one knew why. Whenever someone asked him or mentioned Kenny, his spirit seemed to freeze up.

"It's just wild, Jeremiah," Otis began again. "To wake up every day and know that Kenny is home, not over in Vietnam. Home with us—me, Sam, and Mama. It's just wild." He stared at the ground again. "He promised to take me fishing one weekend, you know, like he used to do."

"Hey, that's good, man," I replied.

Fishing was one of the things Kenny loved. He and Otis used to go down to the creek every Saturday morning with their big red cooler. They would come back with an abundance of fish, which they skinned and gutted for Mrs. Wilson to fry.

"Maybe y'all can catch more of those catfish to eat," I said.

Otis smiled. "Yeah, we could," he said hesitantly. "It's just that . . . there's something wrong with my brother, Jeremiah."

"What do you mean?"

"I don't know how to explain it, but he's not the same as before he left. Sometimes I catch him talking to himself in his room. It's like he's having flashbacks, as if he's back at war. I know he doesn't mean to—it's like he can't help it."

I thought about the time when Kenny was at our house. When Deacon Wallace asked about his time over in Vietnam, I could tell Kenny didn't want to answer.

"He wakes up in the middle of the night, saying he can't sleep," Otis continued. "Then he sometimes goes out and never comes back until the next day."

"What was he doing all that time?" I questioned.

Otis shrugged. "I don't know, but when he comes home, he is different than when he left. He always goes to the bathroom and throws up."

I didn't say anything, just listened.

"He seems angry all the time, angry at everyone. My mom said he may need to see someone to get help, but Kenny said he doesn't need it. I just want my big brother to be normal again. I pray every night he will." He stopped and looked out at the basketball courts. "I guess I better go back and see what everyone's up to before they come looking for me. It was nice rapping with you, Jeremiah. I'll see you in class."

***

"Mama, do you think something is going on with Kenny?" I asked, helping her set up the table for dinner that evening.

Mama looked over at me as I grabbed four plates. "You just need two plates right now, Jeremiah. Your father is shutting in at the church and Ezekiel will be running a bit late practicing."

"You still haven't answered my question, Mama," I said, putting the two plates back. "Do you think something's been going on with Kenny since coming home from the war?"

Mama was mixing the butter into her mashed potatoes to go along with her fried chicken and cornbread.

"He seems like Kenny to me, Jeremiah," she said. She transferred the chicken one piece at a time from the hot grease to a lined plate to drain the excess oil. "What makes you ask that?"

"Because I was talking with Otis today at recess, and he said Kenny sometimes has flashbacks and nightmares from being over in Vietnam."

Mama didn't have the level of surprise I had when Otis told me. I wondered what she's heard.

"He also told me that sometimes Kenny leaves the house at nighttime and doesn't come back for a while, and he's angry at everyone. But he doesn't seem to act differently when we see him."

"Maybe not, Jeremiah," Mama said, her tone serious. "But who knows what Kenny went through over there, just like the rest of those boys who come home. It's going to take time for them to get adjusted to life again."

"But Mama, Otis seems worried. I've never known Otis to worry about anything in his life. He says that he prays for Kenny every night—do you think God will answer his prayer?"

"Of course, he will, Jeremiah," Mama said. "You make sure you do the same and I'm sure everything will be alright in the end for Kenny." She set the food on the table for two. "Now, will you please say grace for the food?" I turned my attention to eating my dinner after I led grace.

***

The next Sunday, amid the middle of the message, Sister Ruth tapped me on the shoulder.

"Jeremiah, can you do me a favor, please?"

I followed her downstairs to the kitchen area when she began telling me that she and Mother Pearl needed my help to set up the communion before service ended for the day. I already knew somewhat where everything was located and how it was arranged on the shiny circular silver platter they bring out every Sunday before the message ends.

"That Pastor McGill knows he's preaching right now, ain't he, Sister Ruth?" Mother Pearl remarked while pouring the grape juice into the cups.

"It is a beautiful sermon so far and a word that is so needed for the body of Christ," Sister Ruth agreed. "The world sure does need more love towards our neighbors. Living in peace and harmony with one another."

"Like the Bible tells us, only the pure in heart shall see God."

"Amen, Mother Pearl," cried Sister Ruth. She looked over at me and asked, "Your father knows he can preach, can't he, Jeremiah?"

"Yes, ma'am," I answered.

"I know he can. That word out there is on time and everything. I wish more preachers were anointed like him."

"I do too," Sister Ruth said while setting out the crackers. "So, tell me something, young man, is your father excited about his church anniversary coming up?"

The church anniversary. Sister Georgia's been announcing the grand event each Sunday since January. Every year around the month of May, our church comes together to celebrate, House of Prayer, Tabernacle of Praise, making it one more year. It was a serious time for the church, with the men dressed in their black suits, dress shirts, and ties, while the women wore long skirts with stockings and stylish hats.

"Yes, ma'am, I think he is," I answered honestly to Sister Ruth.

"That's good," Mother Pearl replied. "I know I can't wait for it. It's going to be a Holy Ghost–filled one. I think I got the menu all ready to go."

"Really? What you plan on cooking?" Sister Ruth asked.

As Mother Pearl was listing all the food she was cooking: fried chicken, ham, macaroni and cheese, sweet corn, dressing, collard greens, cakes, pies, bread pudding, my mouth started to water, especially at the mention of her preparing that famous blueberry pie.

Once we poured out all the juice and Mother Pearl set out the crackers, Sister Ruth sent me to wait by the door leading to the sanctuary. Heading down the hallway, I saw Kenny. I expected him to greet me with his usual beam of joy and happiness but saw something totally different. Kenny was sitting in a chair outside Daddy's office. He was alone, looking like a nervous wreck, rocking himself back and forth. I heard him mumbling some stuff to himself.

I didn't know what he was thinking about that had him all jittery. Whatever it was, it sure was heavy on his mind.

"Kenny?"

He instantly snapped himself out of whatever trance he was in. Seeing me, he forced that contagious personality to come out. It was the freakiest thing I'd ever seen in my life, almost like Dr. Jekyll and Mr. Hyde.

"Say, what's happenin', Jeremiah? I didn't know you were here." His voice had that usual joy in it, but his eyes told another story. It was like staring into a person filled with fear and never-ending terror, almost like death.

"Kenny, are you alright?" I asked softly.

He stood up in an effort to pull himself together. "Who me? I'm solid on down, man," he said, then laughed and added, "Got kind of hot in there with all the good Sunday morning preaching going on from Pastor, right?"

I laughed lightly with him, trying to make the best of the awkward moment, but he could tell I was still worried about him.

"You're looking at me like Otis sometimes looks when he sees me now," he said. "It's like I tell him all the time, Jeremiah. Don't worry about me. I'll be alright." He turned towards the kitchen area. "I hear Mother Pearl and Sister Ruth back there. They must be getting ready for communion."

I nodded. I couldn't help but think Kenny was playing me like a fiddle. We then heard the footsteps of Sister Ruth and Mother Pearl coming out with the crackers and grape juice.

Kenny let out a huge sigh of relief. "How are you doing, Mrs. Sager, Mrs. Ruth?"

"We're doing fine, baby," Sister Ruth answered. "It's good to see you here in the house of the Lord."

"Yes, ma'am," he replied. "Just talking to Jeremiah here, said you all were doing communion today."

"And he did a fine job helping us, just like you used to do when you were younger," Mother Pearl commented. "I haven't really got to talk to you or your family since you got back. Everything going alright for you?"

"Yes, ma'am," he answered again. "Just trying to get back used to this life again, that's all."

"I understand, son. I know your Mama must be one proud lady, with her son coming home from the war a man."

Kenny smiled a little. "Yes, ma'am, I think she is."

"That's good, really good."

When Kenny headed back up to the sanctuary, Mother Pearl turned to Sister Ruth. "I tell you, that boy has grown up on us, hasn't he?"

"He sure has. I still remember when he was just a boy, mowing all our grass in the neighborhood just to make some money to help his mama."

"I always used to tip him a couple of bucks extra because he was so sweet."

Sister Ruth laughed. "Me too, and now he's a handsome young soldier. Judith has got to be one happy mother."

"Jeremiah, are you coming, son?"

"Oh—yes, Mother Pearl."

"Good, because we still need someone to get the door."

CHAPTER 15

SECRETS OF A SOLDIER

One Friday afternoon, I was walking home from school when the old gang caught up to me. They weren't talking about anything much, except Roach was still rambling about seeing Otis in the newspaper. The story was that he scored the big home run during the last inning of the opening-night game.

Since Cape Creek was a small town, news traveled fast. All kinds of kids had come up to Otis that day at school, some wanting his autograph, some—mainly the girls—complimenting the overly shy athlete and giving their phone numbers. Mr. Griffith had approached the celebrity during class, offering his praises of the game. Otis smiled faintly, embarrassed by all the attention.

"Were you nervous when they came to interview you?" Roach playfully asked the superstar-in-training, offering an invisible mic.

Otis leaned into his mic, playing along. "No, I guess I wasn't, really. You know I've got to practice my interviewing skills for when I become a professional athlete," he teased, then added that he was still handing out free autographs for anyone who wanted one.

"Man, Otis, just think, when you become a famous athlete, you have to answer questions, see people all the time, and travel around the world," Drew said. "How will you be able to do it?"

"I don't know, Drew." Otis chuckled. "Colton says that he wants to manage my career, though. He said that all I'm going to have to do is just play the game, and that's it."

"What about me, Otis?" Sam asked. "What am I gonna do?"

"I don't know, Sam," Otis replied. "What do you want to do?"

Sam thought about it, then said, "I want to be your bodyguard when you become famous."

"Bodyguard?" Drew asked. "Sam, do you know what that is?"

"Yup, I get to chase away people that get on Otis's nerves and beat them up."

All of us laughed at the honesty of the seven-year-old boy.

"Say, Otis, you like being with Colton and them white folks more so than us, huh?" Rodney then accused. He looked over at Drew, Roach, and me. "Y'all better look out—Otis may be too good for us to hang tough with."

"Come on, Rodney, let Otis be," Roach said. "You've been on his case all day today about him playing for the Capaha Arrowheads. Sounds like you're a bit jealous."

"Yeah, Rodney, you jealous," Sam chimed in. Otis calmed him down a bit afterward.

"I ain't jealous, Roach," Rodney snapped. "I'm tired of all this talk about Otis Wilson and his great athletic ability. He ain't the only one who can hit a baseball. I mean, I can hit a baseball, too."

"Maybe you can, Rodney, but I bet you can't hit it good enough to be in the paper like Otis can," Roach reminded him.

***

After dinner that evening, Mama went with Ezekiel to the church for choir practice. That left me in the living room with Daddy writing out the scriptures. We had been studying the beatitudes in the fifth chapter of Matthew. I handed Daddy my two sheets of paper to look at. He studied my work as I sat there waiting patiently.

"This is very nicely done, Jeremiah," he approved. "You've come a long way with your writing since we first started."

"Thank you, Daddy."

"I even liked the part where you talked about the meekness of Moses to explain the blessed-are-meek scripture."

Daddy passed the paper back to me. "Well, I think we can call it early for today. Very good work, son."

It was about fifteen minutes later, when I was taking out the trash, that I noticed Kenny down the street. He was coming towards me, waving, and calling out my name.

"What's happening, Jeremiah?"

"Nothing much. How are you?"

"I'm fine, man, just fine," he said. Then he looked inside our open screen door. "Just wanted to see if your dad was home. Figured since I'm in the neighborhood, I'd stop by."

It was kind of strange to see Kenny at that time in the evening. I hoped everything was alright. When I told Daddy who was waiting outside for him, he promptly said he'd be down. So, in his stead, I went out to entertain our guest.

Neither of us said anything, just stared out into the quiet street and enjoyed the cool evening spring breeze. He looked even more different than the last time I saw him. You could still see fear in his eyes.

"It sure is a nice evening out here, ain't it?" Kenny asked.

I nodded my head. "Otis is riding high off of his fame from the paper," I then kidded. "He was signing his autograph in people's notebooks. I even have his John Hancock in my English notebook."

Kenny smiled hugely. "That boy knows he's a true athlete. Can't believe that boy's all grown up, turning twelve years old back in February. I hear he has a lot of girls trying to be his girlfriend now."

I laughed along with him while looking at his newly pressed Bible.

"So, what have you been reading about lately?"

"Oh, nothing in particular, just about Jesus walking on the water. That's one thing I missed when I was in Vietnam—your daddy's teaching of the Word. I just love it when he preaches in service. Don't you?"

"Yeah, he's pretty good. He has me as one of his pupils as well. I didn't like it at first, thought it was boring, but now it's OK."

"I'm glad you think so, Jeremiah. Your dad is a good guy. You're a lot like him, too. Otis has been telling Mom about you."

"Huh? What's he been saying to her?" I asked.

"Well, he's been saying that you know a lot about the Bible and are a good friend, an easy person to talk to. He also said that you're becoming different from all the rest of his friends."

Kenny displayed his excitement for it, while I was still trying to digest all that Otis thought of me. "Hey, hey, man! Otis needs a friend like you. You should be happy about it."

"Well, see, that's the thing. I always saw Otis as the leader of us. I never thought of myself as a cool person."

"I'm hip to what you're saying, man, but Otis and them just don't know how lucky they are to have a friend like you. Oh, hi, Pastor McGill."

I turned around and saw Daddy stepping out of the house. "Kenny, how have you been?"

"I'm alright, Pastor," Kenny responded. "Didn't mean to disturb you or Jeremiah here, but just wanted to come to see you all."

"That's just alright. Everything alright at home?"

"Yes, Pastor."

Daddy smiled. "That's good. Would you like something to eat? I know Carolyn's got plenty left if you want to stay a bit."

"That's OK, Pastor McGill. I know it's kind of late. I need to get going."

"Alright, you take care and tell your mother I said hello."

"Yes, sir," he said.

Daddy then noticed that Kenny was about to leave his newly pressed Bible on the porch. He picked it up and called out to him. "Kenny, don't forget your Bible."

As he handed it to him, Kenny tried to grab it quickly from him. Something fell out and landed on the porch. Daddy reached down to pick it up, then stopped. He began to whisper something under his breath. It sounded like he was praying, speaking in his tongues while keeping his eyes on Kenny the whole time. On the ground was a small bag with white powder-like stuff inside. Kenny finally picked it up and placed it back in his Bible. A weird airless feeling came over me, almost like I couldn't breathe, as I tried to figure out what the stuff was.

Daddy concluded his prayer, letting the wind blow for a minute. "Kenneth," he started. This couldn't be good if Daddy was calling Kenny by his full government name. "Are you sure everything is alright with you?"

Kenny hesitated, not knowing if he should respond to Daddy. He looked back at the spot where the bag had been and then straight at Daddy's eyes. "Come on, Pastor McGill, I'm fine. It ain't nothing to worry about. I promise it ain't. You and Jeremiah here can pretend you never saw it, right?"

"I believe I can't do that, son," Daddy told him. "Kenneth, your mother's worried about you. I was talking to her last week sometime, and she was telling me that maybe it would be a good idea for you to get some help with your experiences in Vietnam—"

"I don't need any help," Kenny quickly answered. "It's just like I told Mom. I can handle this. She may not think I can, but I can, Pastor. Don't look at me like that, Pastor. Please, don't judge me."

"I'm not judging you, Kenneth; you should know better than that. Can you just tell me how long you have been using heroin?"

Heroin?! Kenny has Heroin? Couldn't Be. As Kenny told Daddy that he's been addicted to heroin since fighting over in Vietnam, me and Daddy were forced to face a new reality.

"Does your mother know about it?"

He slowly shook his head. "Otis is the only one who knows. He caught me using it one time in my room."

A lightbulb went off in my head. Everything was making sense now. This was what Otis was trying to tell me at recess that day. I felt my heart sink all the way down to the bottom of my belly as Kenny begged me and Daddy not to tell anyone.

"Son, your mother wants to help you, just like any loving mother would. She needs to know this battle you're dealing with. It's only right for you to tell her."

"You have to understand, Pastor, I . . . I . . . I needed this drug to get me through Vietnam. I was eighteen years old when I was drafted and had to give up everything. I did a lot of things that I am ashamed of. Things you taught me not to do, but I did anyway.

"I come home, and no one sees me the same as before. They call me crazy for fighting in the war. A black token boy for Uncle Sam, and they're right, Pastor. They are right. How can I wake myself up every morning, with those thoughts being over there still in my mind?"

His words were coming out so painfully. He was bearing to us his heavy bleeding soul, what was on his mind, what Otis was afraid of. I guess I never really understood how much the Vietnam War could impact one person, nor could I even imagine all the thoughts running through Kenny's mind every day. It really opened my eyes a lot to the things around me. That there really is a world bigger than Cape Creek, Missouri.

"I gotta get going, Pastor," Kenny said. "Don't y'all worry about me. I can make it."

He began walking off, then Daddy called his name out.

"Kenneth, you may be right that we don't understand what you've been through. A lot of people may see you as a different person, but I know one thing is true: you still have people here that love and care for you. I know your mother loves you, and your brothers adore you. We love you here, and if there is anything you need, never hesitate to ask."

"I appreciate you looking out for me. You and your family always have since our Dad left us."

"And we still will, Kenneth."

"Daddy, what are we gonna do?" I asked when Kenny was gone.

"I don't know, Jeremiah. Your guess is as good as mine."

"I mean, I'm just saying. I never thought Kenny would be one to use drugs."

"Me either, Jeremiah," he agreed. "He was such a bright young man, an honor student. He had such big dreams of being an engineer and making enough money to take care of his family. That boy did everything he set his mind to do. A boy sent off to fight in a big man's war."

As he turned to go inside the house, I had so many questions about Kenny, Vietnam, and heroin. I put my thoughts on hold and was heading into the house when I saw Kenny's Bible, sitting on the side of the porch where he left it.

CHAPTER 16

DAVID AND GOLIATH: A NEW HERO

Otis received after-school detention from Mr. Griffith, which was a big deal because Otis never got detention. Shoot, he'd never been in trouble in all his life. From first grade on up, he had always been the model citizen, honor roll student, prime athlete, hero, Superman. However, something was kryptoniting him. No one had seen or heard from Kenny in three whole days.

With everything happening, it was no wonder Otis was in a numb state of mind while he pushed Sam ahead for school. In class, no one could get over Otis's wall. Mr. Griffith tried to get him to answer a question about the American Revolutionary War during history, but to no avail. He wasn't even paying attention. With all the other kids raising their hands, waiting for him to call on them, Mr. Griffith came back to Otis.

"Otis, I need you to pay attention to this," he reprimanded. "We've got a big history test coming up Friday."

"Yes, sir," he mumbled. I felt Mr. Griffith wanting to break deeper into his wall, but he wisely backed off.

"We're on page seventy-five, Otis," he said instead, with urgency. Otis slowly obeyed, taking out his book from inside his desk, and followed along.

While Mr. Griffith read from the textbook, mainly about the colonists dumping Britain's tea, I stared at the trees rustling in the wind. I could only imagine how Otis must feel, knowing that his oldest brother was addicted to heroin. Lord knows I'd been praying for him, wherever he was. I tried not to think about it too much longer, but instead focused my attention on my sweet love. Christine was always so studious, listening to Mr. Griffith like the wonderful pupil she was. The jitters were all inside of me—my stomach bounced all around like I ate jumping beans—thinking about how pretty she was.

"Jeremiah, what happened on September 3, 1783?"

Not wanting him to think I wasn't paying attention, I quickly stood up and quoted out of thin air: "The peace treaty was signed over in Paris and resulted in George Washington becoming our first president."

"Good," he said.

A few more minutes passed, then Mr. Griffith told us to pass in our essay assignments. He'd posed the topic question sometime last week: "Why did the Founding Fathers fight for our freedoms?" Pulling out my two-page, superbly written paper and passing it to a girl named Sara sitting in front of me, I couldn't help but notice Otis didn't have anything. I worried, seeing that this had become a pattern for Otis lately. He hadn't been doing any of his assignments, I know, for the past week.

It didn't take Mr. Griffith no time to realize that Otis didn't turn in his essay. After he did his normal number check, he slowly shook his head. I kind of ducked my head a little as Mr. Griffith looked over at Otis once again.

"Otis, do you have your essay to turn in?" he inquired.

He didn't answer him, eyes glued to his desk.

"Otis, we've been working on this for about a week now. You've got to have something."

"No, sir, I don't," Otis answered, his eyes still glued to the desk.

"This is the fifth time this week you haven't turned in your homework," Mr. Griffith said, his voice sounding a bit concerned while still unhappy. "Can you at least tell me why you didn't do this assignment?"

Otis, without even so much as raising his head, replied, "Just didn't feel like doing it."

Mr. Griffith tried to talk to him about it some more. "I'm sorry, Otis, but I don't believe that. It isn't like you to miss homework assignments. There has to be something going on that we need to know about."

Still, Otis didn't budge.

Mr. Griffith sighed. "You know my rules, Otis. You'll have to stay after school and do your essay."

There it was, and no one could believe it. There were a couple of gasps and even some small chatter. Colton tried to reason with Otis, even offering to help him do it during recess. If only Mr. Griffith knew why Otis didn't do his homework. I bet you he would've shown some needed mercy towards him. None of it mattered, though, for Otis didn't seem too fazed by any of it.

***

"Are you sure Otis has detention?" Drew asked Colton at recess.

Colton nodded assuredly, standing with us over by one of the two big black basketball goals. "He hasn't been himself at all lately. Not paying attention to Mr. Griffith, mumbling under his breath at times. He hasn't even been turning in his homework. I think that was the last straw for Mr. Griffith."

"Man, I can't believe this," Roach said. "Otis is in real trouble if Mr. Griffith told him he has detention. He's the nice teacher."

"I know," Colton agreed. "He's even missed the last three baseball practices. Dad saw him the other day when he picked me up from school and asked him if everything was alright."

"What did he say?"

"Nothing, really, but just said that he was OK, like what he said to Mr. Griffith today. That's where he is now, talking to him about his behavior."

"I feel mighty bad for Otis right now," Drew said.

"I don't," Rodney said. "It's about time he came down to the level of us commoners."

Rodney had been rubbing me the wrong way for a while. I just couldn't understand it. Usually, I was able to at least tolerate him making fun of people sometimes, or dogging someone out. I even used to laugh at some of his jokes. Now I was getting more and more irritated at him. He didn't even feel the slightest sympathy for Kenny. My vexed spirit watched him take a shot at the basketball goal, hit the backboard, and barely make it. Roach picked up the rebound.

"You know, Otis has never acted like this before, Rodney. He's obviously worried about Kenny."

"What's wrong with Kenny?" Colton asked naively.

We all grew silent, not feeling that responsibility to inform him about Kenny's condition—all except Rodney. He just couldn't wait to open his mouth and tell him everything. Out of all the times Rodney could've had a conversation with Colton, this was when he made sure to slither his way over. He'd almost succeeded in poisoning his mind when Roach looked up and said, "Hey, Otis!"

We all looked up and saw Otis walking towards us. I looked for some indication that Mr. Griffith may have shown some leeway toward him, but he showed nothing. He asked Drew to make sure Sam got home from school today as he motioned for the ball from Roach, then dribbled around the foul line.

"Well, well, looks like the mighty, great Otis Wilson has detention today after school, huh?"

Otis dribbled the basketball a bit more before making a clean shot inside the goal as we watched. The sound of a swish was his answer.

Rodney walked towards him; a bit agitated. "So, you're not gonna say anything now?" he questioned, while taking the basketball forcefully from him. "You still think you're too good to talk to us, don't you?"

"I don't think anything, Rodney," Otis said calmly. He grabbed the ball back and instantly made another shot inside the goal.

"Say, guys, we got enough people to play a quick pickup game before recess ends," Colton proposed.

Everyone seemed all for it, including Otis. They picked out teams and ignored Rodney. That really made him mad. He was losing his audience over Otis—again. He took a big step forward, and like a dragon about to breathe fire, he puffed out his chest and fired his shot. "Say, Colton, I never did get to tell you about Otis's brother, Kenny, did I?"

Otis froze, and the ball dropped out of his hand. He slowly glanced over at Rodney, who had this emotionless look on his face. He'd not only gained Otis's attention but got his audience back, too. Knowing this, he decided to land another strike.

"I mean, you always hang with us now, and like all friends that hang, you should know about Otis's dear, perfect brother Kenny."

"Aww, come on, Rodney, let up, will ya?" said Drew. "Colton doesn't need to know what's going on with Otis."

"Who asked you to talk?" Rodney snapped. Drew clammed up. Rodney then turned back to Otis. "Besides, what I'm sayin' ain't nothing but the truth. Right, Otis?"

Otis, with tears welling up in his eyes, balled up his fists. This was it. Otis was going to strike Rodney any second, but he didn't care.

Rodney was too busy feeling himself like a peacock in full bloom. His mouth was in stride and there was nothing to stop him.

"Since Colton here is your friend, it should be no secret that your brother is a drug addict on heroin."

"On drugs?" Colton then questioned. "That's not true, is it?"

"Of course it's true," Rodney quickly answered. "Everyone knows it. Why do you think he hasn't been coming to y'all practices or is all of a sudden acting distant? He just don't want any of us to find out that his life ain't perfect."

Colton had the same look of heaviness we all shared. It looked like he was about to say something, but Rodney didn't give him a chance. He was too busy sneering down at Otis.

"Shoot, I bet you Kenny's probably somewhere going around begging for money for his next high."

Otis's power was down to almost nothing. I began to do something I always saw my parents do at times like this—pray. I prayed that the bell would ring for us to line up or maybe one of the teachers would come over and bring some peace. I even prayed for Rodney's mouth to stop talking, even though we all knew that would be in vain.

"Tell me something, Otis," Rodney began, going for the kill. "How does it feel that your brother used to be an all-city basketball player and is now an embarrassment to the black community? He ain't nothing more than a half-assed GI junkie."

"Rodney, stop! Leave Otis alone!"

Everyone immediately turned to face me as I tried to figure out who inside of me spoke. I didn't know if it was me or my father. A strength came over my voice that no one had ever heard before. It was like when I said "Leave Otis alone" to Rodney, I meant it.

"We're tired of you messing with him," I explained further. "It just ain't right for you to talk about Kenny and his situation. Just like it ain't right for you to call Colton Casper or boss Drew around from time to time."

"Really? Who's gonna stop me, huh, preacher's kid?" Rodney asked daringly. By now, I guess everyone thought that I would back down, not wanting to start a conflict. But that didn't happen this time. Something inside of me wasn't scared. It wasn't scared of Rodney; it wasn't scared of anyone at that moment. The same superstrength usually on Otis, somehow jumped onto me as I actually came toe-to-toe with Rodney and replied, "I am."

"Ooooooo-wee! Jeremiah's coming for you now, Rodney," Roach said.

As I stood there, I realized I'd never really looked at the difference in size between myself and Rodney. When we first started the sixth grade, Rodney was taller than me. Now, we were both twelve and about the same height. He didn't have the reach on me like before. In fact, I could probably get in a good wallop or two. Lord knows I didn't want to fight Rodney, but I did want him to leave Otis alone.

Trying to keep his ego intact, Rodney laughed like Goliath would to keep up his bravery. "Yeah right. The Preacher Kid ain't gonna do nothin'. Everyone knows he's weak and can't fight."

"Oh yeah? Well, why don't you hit me and find out how weak I am?"

No one seemed to move at that point as they tried to figure out if I was serious or not. I was bold like David. I looked at Drew while Roach egged for a spring fight between me and Rodney.

"You heard Jeremiah, Rodney," Roach said, staring at Rodney. "Go on and hit him."

Rodney quickly raised his fist and struck close to the left side of my face to see if I would flinch. When I didn't move but stood my ground, I thought he was about to connect a second punch right square on my jaw, but that didn't happen. Rodney slowly let down his fist. Realizing there was no backing down, Rodney had to change his tune.

He smiled, then tried slick-talking his way out of this embarrassing situation. "I see that the church boy got more guts than I thought," he said. "Too bad my mom said if I get sent to Mr. Burns one more time, it's my hide. Or else I'd knock you out in a couple of rounds."

I couldn't believe it. After all these years, I finally stood up to Rodney Turner. I didn't know whether to smile or give myself a pat on the back. One thing was for sure, it definitely felt good to get the upper hand for once.

After the dust settled, we looked at Otis. Our superhero was still picking up the pieces of what just happened. He slowly lifted his head to face us as a tear ran slowly down his cheek. For the first time in my life, I actually felt so sorry for Otis. He wasn't our superhero who defended us from evil. This time, it was he that needed to be saved.

Drew was the first one to speak to our broken friend. "Otis, don't worry about Rodney. Kenny's gonna be alright."

Colton tried again to force a smile out of Otis by cracking one of his funny yet corny jokes. That did bring out a slight grin, even if no one else got the punch line. We started to walk away to enjoy what was left of our recess, then Otis finally spoke.

"Jeremiah," he called, softly.

"Yeah, Otis," I answered, turning back.

Otis looked over at me. "Thanks, man," he said. "Thanks."

"Don't worry about it, man," I replied. "You've bailed us out so many times, so I just returned the favor. That's what friends do for each other."

"I just wish Kenny would come off drugs," Otis then said, to the point of almost sobbing. "I want my family back to normal again."

My left hand reached out towards him, gently placing it on his head as if I was Daddy on Sunday morning. Just like my old man, I said a small prayer for my friend, his brother, and their family. I prayed that Kenny would come home. I prayed that he would be alright. I prayed that Otis would have his family back to normal again.

CHAPTER 17

THE CALL

"**D**rew, what is Matthew 5:3?"

Drew stood up and delivered the answer. "Blessed are the poor in spirit, for they shall inherit the earth. Matthew 5:3."

We'd been practicing and preparing all Saturday afternoon and evening up in the choir stand, going over all that we were going to do for the church anniversary coming up in the middle of May. I couldn't tell you how many times Sister Ruth made us sing or Zeke played those same songs on that organ. We recited the same nine beatitude scriptures over and over again until it was oozing out of our ears.

Now came the final step, assigning all the roles we had to fill. Sister Ruth was going down her list of the services performed by adults every Sunday, like ushers, announcers, door greeters, and offering officials. So far, Sister Ruth didn't have any problem getting volunteers, until it was time to assign the last role.

"Alright now, young ministers," she said, quieting us down. "I'm going to need someone to do the most important job—delivering a sermon for that evening. Does anybody feel led by God to take on that responsibility?"

She looked around the room and saw not one other person showing interest. "Nobody? Nobody at all?"

She scanned around the room once more. "How about you, Jeremiah? I don't have you down for anything."

Sister Ruth checked her list over and over, and she was right. In the rush of everyone else taking their assignments, Sister Ruth had almost overlooked me.

"Would you like to say something at the anniversary, Jeremiah? I think your father and mother would love that."

"Yeah, Jeremiah, why don't you do it?" Drew said. Roach even began trying to boost me up. Even Zeke rooted for me. They didn't really have to, because truth be told, I was hoping Sister Ruth would ask me to speak.

When I told her yes, Sister Ruth beamed, glad that I would preach my first sermon. Sister Ruth lifted her hand up, gesturing for everyone to be silent again. "Alright, now it's settled. I got Jeremiah McGill as the speaker of the night. The Pastor and First Lady are going to be so proud."

***

I knew if I was going to be ready to speak for Youth Night, I had to get started now. I had two whole weeks. Three days had passed, and I had nothing. For everyone saying that I had a writing ability beyond my years, this was my hardest assignment yet. Nothing was coming to me that made sense. Throughout my search for scripture after scripture, I couldn't come up with anything that I could write down.

Every evening, I heard Zeke pass by in the hallway, signaling to me that dinnertime was almost here.

"You still working on your sermon, Jeremiah?" he would ask, peering over my shoulder every time he walked to my desk.

"Uh-huh," I would reply.

"Still ain't got nothing."

"Uh-uh."

"Just keep writing, it'll come to you."

I'd watch him walk off, then look down at all the scribbles of jumbled words.

The night before when he came by, I was so desperate for some headway that I asked him how he would write the sermon. He acted as if he didn't even want to tell me.

"Don't be so hard on yourself, Jeremiah," he said. "If it was me preaching, I'm sure I'd be going through the same thing you're going through right now."

I shook my head. "I don't see how Daddy can write messages almost every week without even thinking about it hard," I commented. "It's like he has messages for days at a time."

"Aww, it's easy for Pop, li'l bro. He's been doing this since he was a young buck. Here's the skinny that I'll tell you. Pop told me one time that sometimes, when he writes his messages, they come off as inspiration."

"Inspiration?"

"Yeah, man, inspiration. You know, stuff that inspires you, gets you going."

"Zeke, I'm just a kid. I don't know what inspires me."

"Well, li'l bro, I wish I could help you right now, but you should be happy you're doing this. You know, Pop is ecstatic."

"Yeah, sure," I said, feeling even more pressure.

I decided to give myself a break from racking my brain with this whole writing-down-a-message thing. I went to the kitchen, where Mama was pulling something out of the oven. She also asked me for an update.

"Not good," I admitted. "Mama, I have nothing written down for Youth Night. Everyone is depending on me to have the message, just like Daddy."

"Oh Jeremiah, you're just putting a lot of pressure on yourself," she told me. "You can't base your message on what Walter has. You have to find your own message, what God is saying to you."

"But how do I find my own message?"

"Just keep on doing what you're doing. You're seeking God, fasting, and praying. He'll speak to you, and I'm sure whatever sermon he gives you will be perfect for us to hear."

Then, about two days later, everything finally started to come together. It started with this scripture in the Bible that stuck with me, saying, "Before I formed you in the womb I knew you, and before you were born, I consecrated you; I have appointed you a prophet to the nations." I didn't know why I gravitated toward that particular scripture. Probably because it came from the same book of the Bible that I was named after. When I kept reading further, the passage really came alive inside of me, especially the part when God told Jeremiah not to be afraid, for he would always be with him.

By the time I was finished, I had a sermon on my hands. It wasn't perfect, but it was better than the scribbles and doodles that were on my page before.

"Aww, Zeke, tell me what you think?"

I found him sitting in the living room practicing on the piano some of the songs for the anniversary. I explained the situation, about finding my inspiration to write, just like Daddy. Of course, being Zeke, he prolonged his reading time, acting as if he was intensely reading my work.

"Come on, Zeke. It's only a few pages of writing. You act as if you're reading a whole book or something."

"Judging work takes time, li'l bro," he said. "Now, you want a professional opinion, right?"

I had no choice but to sit there and wait. From how long Zeke took to read, it was going to take ten minutes for him to review one line. After he cleared his throat about three times, he finally said something.

"Wow, li'l bro, I ain't gonna lie. This is a pretty out-of-sight sermon. Even the title's on point. Sounds like something Pop would write."

I felt a little proud of my writing when Zeke said that. He said it reminded him of one of Daddy's pieces, which was the ultimate compliment for a writer. I grabbed my pages from him and read to myself as Zeke walked to the kitchen. When he came back into the living room with this big bowl of macaroni and cheese from dinner.

Listening to me practice, pretending I was up there preaching my sermon on the mount, he stopped eating and asked, "Are you nervous yet?"

I looked over at him. He was basically devouring his third helping of macaroni without Mama knowing. "I don't know. I don't feel like I'm nervous."

"Good," Zeke said. He scarfed the rest of his food down before adding, "I just hope you ain't gonna sound like some of the others that stand up there and speak."

"Sound like what?" I questioned.

"You know, boring and dry," he answered, setting his bowl down on the long glass table in front of him. "You've written a great message, Jeremiah, and I mean it's a *great* message. But it takes more than a great message to win over a crowd. You remember Clarence."

Boy, did I ever. Clarence Gregory Johnson had given a sermon three years before, during our youth services. He was Mother Pearl's nephew, a nice fellow who loved to read the Bible and had good ideas about God, but he was always hard to listen to. He had this nasal, high-pitched voice that would always crack when he got nervous. Lord knows I didn't want to be like that up there speaking. Especially in front of my parents and family.

"Zeke, you think I would do good next Friday, you know, for a twelve-year-old speaking for the first time?" I asked.

I thought he would take his time answering, just like he did reading my work, but instead he promptly answered. "For sure, li'l bro, you're gonna do great."

"But what if I mess up and forget one of my words? What if I speak too fast where no one would understand me? What if I speak too slowly? What if I get cotton mouth like Clarence did?"

Zeke burst out in laughter, basically blowing off my concerns. "Trust me, Jeremiah, you're sitting on a gold mine with this sermon."

"Really? You think I'll really do great?" I said. "You think Mama and Daddy would be proud?"

Zeke crossed his heart. "Listen, Jeremiah, you just get up there and drive this message home like Daddy would. With me playing behind you, everyone is gonna be on their feet. It'll be like an old-fashioned revival coming from a twelve-year-old. Did you do what Sister Ruth told us since our last rehearsal?"

Sister Ruth gave us the task of inviting all the people we knew to our service on next Friday night. Basically, she wanted us to invite all our friends and family to church. I told Zeke that I, in fact, invited all my friends at school this past week. The news of me giving my first sermon stoked some sort of intrigue in everyone. I kind of felt like a school celebrity for the first time, only I was too preoccupied to bask in it.

"What about Christine?" Zeke then asked me.

The confidence I'd gained all of a sudden dwindled down. Zeke knew Christine was the one person I wanted to invite more than anyone. She was the one person I would love to sit in the front row, wearing one of her beautiful skirts with her hair in a nice glowing Afro, being impressed by my way with words. I mean, we had been spending a lot of time together this school year like we did back when we were younger. Trouble was, I still didn't know if she would give me the time of day.

When Zeke asked me about Christine again, I came up with an answer, sort of.

"Well, I want to invite her," I said, trying to think of an excuse not to. I was hoping Zeke would give me one, but he pushed me to invite her.

"What's the holdup?" he asked. "You know you want her to come."

I shrugged anxiously. "Yeah, I do."

"And you know you like her—a lot—right?"

"I know that, Zeke."

"You need to stop being a chicken and ask her to come," he said.

"I ain't too chicken," I said. "Christine's just a different girl, that's all."

"How so?" asked Zeke. "All you gotta do is go up to her and ask her to church. Simple as that."

"It's not that simple, Zeke, not for me, at least," I admitted. "I mean, what if she says no?"

"Well, what if she says yes?" he questioned back. "You never know what will happen if you daydream about it all the time."

I had to think about what Zeke was saying and weigh all the options. For one thing, he was right that I always fantasize about my love for Christine. Maybe it was time for me to break out of my fantasy and finally tell Christine how I feel.

"All I'm saying, li'l bro, is that you have to take that chance. You might be surprised by what Christine would say. Next week is the anniversary." Zeke went back to practicing again, but not before he winked over at me and added, "Besides, if she does say no, it would be her loss, not yours."

CHAPTER 18

JEREMIAH McGILL, THE LOVER

I had decided to take Zeke's advice and finally mustered enough courage to ask the prettiest girl in school to church. My notebook was filled with different scenarios that could play out. I had even come up with a poem to read to her. It said:

Christine,
Refreshing and cool, love is like the morning dew when I see you
Love is like springtime with your eyes sparkling like the stars in the sky
A bird chirps so sweetly,
To tell of the love I have for you deeply
My love is like gold, for the whole world to know
That I genuinely love you
More and more each day

I would stare at myself in the bathroom mirror each night, practicing some of the facial poses celebrities do. I'd take my glasses off, smile all romantic-like and create this deep voice Sidney Poitier could've used. One time, I got into the act so much that I set an actual romantic love scene in my head like you might see on television. Everything was like one of those classic black-and-white movies from the roaring twenties.

Christine was sitting in this big, tall mansion surrounded by all kinds of boys, Rodney included, who was asking for her hand in courtship. Sure, they would give all kinds of lines and speeches on how they would love to take her out, and she would turn them all down.

"I'm sorry, boys," she would tell them. "I'm looking for that one special boy to take my heart away."

It seemed as if all hope was lost until she saw me getting out of this white car. Everyone would freeze as I walked up to her all cool-like, a slow jazz song with a trumpet solo preparing the way in the background.

"Who's that guy?" one would ask.

"I don't know, but he sure looks familiar," another would say.

"Aww, it ain't nobody but Jeremiah," Rodney would reveal.

"Whoever he is, he sure has that charm."

I'd go up to her, ask her for her hand, and get down on one knee to profess my love with my poem in my deep voice.

"Oh, Jeremiah, that's beautiful," she would say, all princess-like.

"Would you like to dance with me?"

Every other person would be fading in the background as a distant memory to both of our minds until it was just me and her dancing together. As the trumpets began to crescendo, she would fall in love with me. Then, slowly, her lips would reach out for one kiss. I'd respond by meeting her lips halfway with mine. Closer, closer, closer than we—

I opened my eyes and noticed my lips puckered on the mirror as if I were kissing Christine. I hurried and woke myself up, grabbed a piece of tissue and wiped my lip print off the mirror, and walked out like nothing happened.

The next day came. Mr. Griffith was still writing yesterday's math problems on the board, so I quickly put my things inside my desk and looked around for Christine. When I spied her heading to the hallway with Susie, I gave myself a push over that way. I even made sure my shirt was tucked in and straight. Zeke had said that girls always loved first impressions, especially the wardrobe.

In the hallway, I stayed close to the two girls, who were whispering and talking. If I was going to talk to Christine, it had to be with no one around. Once she was by herself at the water fountain. The time was right; the moment was now, and I had my lines together. I put on a cool, manly walk and made my way to her.

I wiped down my glasses and smiled. "Hi, Christine."

"Hi, Jeremiah," she replied.

"So, nice weather out here, huh?"

What kind of conversation starter is that?

"Uh-huh," she agreed.

Nice save, Jeremiah.

"Our church is having our anniversary and we kids are presenting a service."

"Oh, that's wonderful."

"Yeah, I have to be one of the people who give a short sermon."

She smiled. "I'm sure you're gonna do great."

Read the poem. Read the poem now, before it's too late!

I had to get myself back into reality. I pulled out my opus. As Zeke said, it was now or never.

"Christine, I want to read something to you."

She was all ears when I announced that it was a poem. I was shaking like a leaf on a tree. I imagined the same scene I'd set when I was alone in the bathroom, filled with music and all. That calmed me down a bit.

Alright, here's your chance, Jeremiah. Don't screw this up.

"Christine," I began to read. "Refreshing and cool, love is like the morning dew when I see you. Love is like the springtime with your eyes sparkling like the stars in the sky. A bird chirps so sweetly, to tell of the love I have for you deeply. My love is like gold, for the whole world to know. That I genuinely love you, more and more each day."

"Oh, that was beautiful, Jeremiah," Christine said.

"You think so?"

"I loved it," she said. "Was that all for me?"

"Yes," I told her. "I wanted to tell you how much I like you and wanted to ask you, if you're not doing anything—"

The morning bell.

Oh no. That meant my time with Christine was ending. I hadn't gotten down on one knee yet. What was I going to do? The plan wouldn't work unless I got down on one knee to complete it. Mr. Griffith was calling both our names from the doorway of the classroom, so I had to think of something, fast.

"Christine, I was wondering if you would like to come to our church service this Friday, if you're not too busy."

She didn't respond at first but turned to look at me even as Mr. Griffith said, "Let's go, you two!"

"I mean, I was just wondering if you wanted to. You know I'm speaking by myself that evening, and it would mean a lot if you would come," I said as we made our way back to class. She still didn't respond, which led me to believe she didn't want to. It was time for damage control and saving what was left of my dignity.

That's when she told me the answer every boy wants to hear. "I'd love to, Jeremiah."

"You would?" I quickly asked.

When she nodded, my spirit leaped for joy. I was on cloud nine. Just think, Christine Hill said yes to me, Jeremiah McGill. Of course, we had to ask her grandfather, Mr. Remington, but that didn't bother me. I was still caught up in the fact that Christine actually wanted to accompany me to church on Friday. Can you believe it? I couldn't. For the rest of the school day, nothing or no one could bring me down.

***

I couldn't wait to tell Zeke the good news that evening. I owed him that much since he was the one who pushed me to invite her. Everything in my mind was in such a high adrenaline rush. I still couldn't believe that I asked Christine out. It had to have been close to ten o'clock at night when he finally made it to his room.

"You still ain't asleep yet?" he asked calmly.

"I can't," I said. "Zeke, you wouldn't believe it, man."

"Believe what?"

"I'm talking about today at school, what happened to me, and Christine." I tried to wait for him to ask more but couldn't hold it any longer. "She said yes, Zeke."

"She did, huh?" he exclaimed, more in his big brother's tone.

"I'm still kind of shocked that she's coming," I commented.

Zeke smiled. "You're gonna do so good preaching that all your friends are gonna be envious and the girls are gonna want to talk to you. Don't be surprised if Christine wants to kiss you."

"Kiss me? I don't think that's going to happen, Zeke." I said.

"Hey, trust me li'l bro, you never know. You ain't too young to receive your first kiss. I was 12 years old when I had mine."

"You did? From who?"

"It happened at the church picnic one summer," Zeke began. "It was with this girl named Joan."

"Joan? I don't know anybody named Joan from the church."

"Well, she used to live here and go to our church back in the day. She moved away when I was about thirteen. She liked me and I kind of liked her. We were hanging down at the creek all by ourselves, just talking and things like that, when suddenly out of nowhere she reached over and kissed me on the lips."

"What did you do?"

"What else was I supposed to do? I kissed her back."

"Did you like it?"

"I don't know, Jeremiah. We kissed for a good while, and at the time I thought it was nice, but looking back at it, that was the chappiest kiss ever. It didn't even feel like love, and I felt no sparks at all. If you do kiss Christine on the lips, make sure that your breath is right and your lips ain't chappy."

I chuckled, and Zeke laid back down.

He was trying to give me some more of his brotherly wisdom but was drifting off into sleep. I sat by his door and listened to him finally give in to the sandman, yet I couldn't sleep a wink. All I could think about was Christine.

When I finally fell asleep in my room, some small noises and chatter awakened me. It sounded like it was coming from downstairs. Reaching for my glasses, I glanced over at the clock sitting on my desk. It was 3:19 in the morning. I sat up, wondering who in the world would be over at our house at the time of night. Not able to go back to sleep, I climbed out of bed and stumbled over to Zeke's room, thinking maybe it was him who was up. He was still knocked out cold.

I walked downstairs, following the familiar voice. The light was on in the kitchen. Creeping slowly, I was able to hear Daddy's voice. He was talking to someone, but I couldn't really make out who. I peeked around the corner and found Daddy in his robe, sitting at the table. Across from him was another person—Kenny. Kenny was over at our house, and it looked like he was eating.

"First Lady knows she can cook a roast, can't she, Pastor?"

Daddy laughed a bit, then answered. "Yes, Kenny, she can."

From what I could see, Kenny was eating some of our leftovers like it was going to be his last supper. He took down bite after bite, only drinking a bit of lemonade from time to time. I didn't know how he could eat all of that and not choke.

"Slow down, son," Daddy urged. "The food's not going anywhere." Kenny lifted his head to acknowledge Daddy. He did take a drink after that before slowly starting on his helping of collard greens. He took each bite a bit slower as Daddy studied his face.

"Looks like you got into a bit of a scuffle tonight?" he asked. Kenny stopped eating, bowing his head with respect to Daddy as he quietly answered. "Yes, sir, I did."

"Better clean that up." Daddy stood up and walked over to the refrigerator. He pulled out an ice tray with some cubes in it. He put a few cubes into a small bag and carefully placed the bag on Kenny's face.

"I'm sorry for comin' over this time of night, Pastor," Kenny said, a bit remorseful. "But I just didn't know who else to turn to."

"That's alright," Daddy said. "We've been worried about you. Wondering where you've been."

Kenny chuckled a bit and took the bag from Daddy. "I've kind of been all around, you know? Sikeston, Charleston, Cairo." He looked down, ashamed. "I messed up bad, didn't I, Pastor?"

"What makes you say that?"

"You know, Pastor, about my addiction. What I did to Mom and my family, stealing and pawning her wedding ring? I know people are talking—probably shouldn't be here at all right now."

"Nonsense," Daddy replied. "You're in the right place. I'm glad that you're alright."

Daddy sat back to let Kenny eat some more. A few seconds later, Daddy posed another question. "Kenny, I know your folks would want to see you in person?"

"No," Kenny said. "I can't go back there, Pastor. I can't let them see me like this. I'm no good to her or my brothers."

"Kenny, you haven't been home in almost a week and a half. You can't stay out there forever. You're too good for that, and those drugs have done nothing for you. Kenny, I know you are dealing with a lot, but please, let us help you."

In the past, when people offered to help Kenny, he shot them down instantly. This time, his posture was more subdued. Although he contemplated whether to accept Daddy's offer, his answer was still the same. "I want to, Pastor, but I gotta figure this out myself."

Having no choice but to accept Kenny's answer, Daddy reached inside Mama's jar beside the cabinet and pulled out a couple of ten-dollar bills. "Then, I want you to take this."

Kenny was reluctant. "No, Pastor, I can't take it."

"Please, Kenny, take it."

Daddy placed the money in Kenny's hand. Kenny bowed his head with humility. "I'm gonna pay you back, Pastor. I promise I'm going to."

"Don't worry about paying me back. I just want you to see your family. I want you to get better. Promise me you will do that." Kenny nodded slowly. "It's alright, Jeremiah, you can come in."

As I came into the cold kitchen, Kenny turned to see me. I was able then to get a good look at him. I almost fell back a bit in shock. He looked so sick and was thinner. His eyes looked even stranger than before, almost like death. He smelled as if he hadn't bathed in days. I had never seen Kenny Wilson like this. I was scared for him. I was scared for his life.

"Hey, preacher man!" he cried.

Standing over beside Daddy I spoke back to Kenny. "How have you been Kenny?"

"Your father was just talking about you," he said. "How you gonna be preaching for the anniversary. I know you're gonna do great."

"Maybe you can come and watch Kenny," I said. "You always said you'd love to hear me speak like my father."

Kenny nodded and grinned. "You're right Jeremiah, you're right. Maybe I will come to watch you." He finished his lemonade, leaving the leftovers. "I better get going, Pastor. Don't wanna overstay my welcome. Tell Mrs. McGill that was some good pot roast she cooked."

Me and Daddy watched Kenny walk out the front door and disappear into the night. I really hoped to see Kenny at the Church Anniversary. Something inside of me felt that if he would come, everything would be alright for him and Otis. I pondered the thought quietly as Daddy began cleaning up after himself and Kenny. Maybe he would come. Maybe he wouldn't. In the end, I said a quick prayer to myself about it when Daddy instructed me to go back to bed.

CHAPTER 19

THE CHURCH ANNIVERSARY OF '72

The church anniversary was here. The atmosphere at House of Prayer, Tabernacle of Praise, was in the spirit of jubilee. Everything and everyone seemed to come alive. The decorations of purple and white around the church were festive and had a sense of royalty. The music was going to sound good, with Zeke shining bright on that organ and the choir singing like heavenly angels. Mama and Daddy will be sitting in kingly and queenly chairs made especially for this occasion upon the pulpit. The congregation was on such a spiritual high.

While I was getting ready for the service, I looked over my outfit. Sister Ruth had told us boys to wear white shirts and black pants, and the girls had to wear white tops and red skirts. I wanted to wear a suit, more to impress Christine than anything else. Having laid my black suit coat and pants, white shirt, and red tie out on my bed, I noticed I had a few minutes before we'd leave for church. I picked up my sermon from the nightstand and read over it a few more times. Using an Afro pick left on my desk as a microphone, I started to read, pretending I was Daddy giving his sermon on a Sunday morning.

"We Give an honor to God, and everyone in their respective places," I said. "Truly, it's a privilege to stand here today, to present to you the words of the Lord."

That sounded good. Professional—and smart. I could hear in my mind the chords Zeke sometimes played on the organ when

Daddy was greeting the saints. I kept on reading, starting again from the beginning of my sermon.

"Saints of God, I want you to turn in your Bibles to Jeremiah chapter one," I recited. "Around the fourth verse, it reads 'The word of the Lord came to me, saying, before I formed you in the womb I knew you, before you were born, I set you apart.'"

I said some more stuff, then around halfway through my practice round, I noticed something happening. My talking slowly turned into preaching, the way Daddy sometimes did. I was singing, jumping around, and praising God in front of an imaginary audience—or so I thought. I was so in my own world that I didn't even see or hear Mama standing behind me in the doorway. When I turned around from dancing and shouting, she was covering her mouth and shaking with laughter.

I came out of my imagination in a hurry. "Sorry, Mama, I guess I got a bit carried away."

"No, no, no," Mama said, still laughing a bit. "No need to apologize for practicing your sermon."

"Yes, ma'am," I said, putting the Afro pick back on my desk.

"Seems to me that you're ready to preach tonight, huh?"

"Yes, ma'am," I said once more. "I don't know how I feel. I mean, one part of me is excited because I have never done something like this before, and the other part is scared."

She let herself in and sat beside my clothes on the bed. She looked ready to go, wearing a white blouse and red skirt, her red hat in her hand. "I know how you feel, Jeremiah," she said. "I can imagine your father felt the same way when he first preached."

"How old was he when he spoke for the first time?"

Mama began thinking. "Oh, not much younger than you— about ten years old the first time I saw him preach. It's funny you asked because I remember that day so well. Walter *looked* like a ten-year-old boy standing behind the podium at the pulpit. He had on this nice brown pair of trousers with a white shirt, his hair slicked back a bit, and those too-big glasses, but when he opened his mouth to preach, he spoke with wisdom and knowledge, like a grown man."

I nodded, looking at Mama. She had this weird, motherly look towards me, one that I'd never seen before.

"Mama, what's wrong?" I asked.

"Oh, nothing," she said, maintaining that overly motherly look. "I got a call from Mr. Remington before I came up here. He said he's coming to church tonight, and you invited their granddaughter, Christine."

"Yes, ma'am," I said, feeling a bit embarrassed.

She didn't say anything at first. I didn't know what would happen next, but alas, she let out a huge smile. "Oh Jeremiah, I think that's so sweet of you. Asking that nice girl Christine out to church this evening," she cried, beaming. "I remember when she and her grandfather used to live around the corner from us. She's blossoming into a nice young lady. Zeke told me you like her."

"He did?" I cried. "That boy knows he has a mouth too big for his head."

"Well, it wasn't hard to figure out that you were fond of her, Jeremiah, since we were neighbors at one time."

"You could tell then?"

Mama smiled slyly. "Let's just say a mother always knows her children. I think it would be good for her to hear you speak tonight."

"I hope I do good enough that she would like it," I said.

"I believe you will, Jeremiah," Mama predicted. "Don't be surprised if she starts to be fond of you too, especially after she sees you up there. That's what happened to your father when he started preaching at a young age."

"Are you saying that could happen to me and Christine?" I asked.

She laughed. "Christine is a very nice young lady, Jeremiah. She would make a fine young wife someday."

"Wife?" I cried. "I'm not thinking about a wife right now. We just passed the sixth grade."

"Oh, you'll start thinking about it sooner than you think, son," she said. "Before you know it, you'll find the right girl, get married, and have your own family to raise."

I smiled over at her. "And then you'd be a grandma, Grandma Carolyn."

"Let's not rush that part, now," she said. "One day, I will be a grandmother to you and Ezekiel's children, but hopefully not too soon."

"Yes, Mama," I said.

She stood up and walked to the door, then turned to look at me. "You're gonna do wonderful tonight, Jeremiah. Everyone is going to be so proud, just like me and your father. Our two young men that's in the church. That'll make anyone proud."

***

The first part of the service seemed to be long and drawn out. All of us young people ministering were waiting in the foyer. They clumped together the girls on one side, dressed in white blouses and red skirts; the boys were scattered on the other side, dressed in white tops and black pants. I spotted Drew and Roach, both wearing their white shirts tucked snugly inside their black trousers. They looked at me and their mouths kind of dropped.

Roach was the first one to speak. "Wow, Jeremiah, you got them preacher threads on tonight, don't ya?"

Drew nodded. "Yeah, Jeremiah, you do look like a real minister compared to the rest of us."

"Thanks," I replied, now feeling overdressed in my full-fledged suit and tie and my Bible by my side. "You all look nice tonight as well," I quickly added, trying to make them feel a bit better.

Talking with Drew and Roach helped take my mind off all the people that were coming inside. Not only had the different saints from Sunday to Sunday come out, but so had folks who used to be members here but had moved away, such as Mr. and Mrs. Battles and their kids—all nine of them. They were all wide-eyed and in happy spirits talking to Sister Ruth about the service tonight. We also had the chance to talk with Otis a bit, who was with his mom, Sam, and Kenny. He was in better spirits, especially since Kenny came home, and promised that he was going to get help. That actually made me smile, that God answered our prayers.

I saw a lot of kids from around the city that Sister Ruth had told us to invite. I didn't see Christine just yet, but there was Rodney with his folks. Colton and his dad showed up. A few more kids I knew came in, but no Christine.

With more people entering the building close to our start time, Sister Ruth gathered us all into one big clump of twenty-five kids and teenagers. She was a big stickler for starting on time. Everything had to be done decently and in order.

I listened to her talk, still looking for Christine to show up. When Sister Ruth came across me, her mouth dropped.

"Jeremiah McGill, don't you look very handsome tonight," she said. "I'm sure you are ready to preach tonight?"

"Yes, Sister Ruth, I think I am."

She warmly and graciously nodded, then finished lining us all up.

As Zeke started playing our first song, "We Are Soldiers in the Army of the Lord," we marched in from the back of the church. We were sounding good, just like Zeke taught us in rehearsal, probably

better, and the routine was going as planned. Even though I was
enjoying the singing, I was looking out into the crowd. There were
a lot of people coming to see us young people, but no Christine. I
just hoped she hadn't changed her mind—or what if she went to the
wrong church? Mama said she'd talked to Mr. Remington, so they
had to know where the church was.

When the offering of the evening was taken up, Sister Ruth
went up to the pulpit to say a few words. The crowd was still engaged,
and more people were coming in from the back. There she was!
Christine was walking in with her grandpa. She had on that emerald-
green skirt and black shoes, and her hair was slicked down to her
shoulders. She came—she actually came, and she sat in the middle
row, right where I'd imagined she'd sit. When she waved at me, I felt
almost queasy inside.

I didn't have time to dwell on the feeling, because it wasn't
too much longer before Sister Ruth called my name. This was it. I
couldn't turn back now. I walked to the pulpit and looked out into
the congregation. They had smiles on their faces, and all they saw on
mine was nerves. I set my notes on the podium along with my Bible
and took two deep breaths.

"Praise the Lord, everybody."

"Praise the Lord," they replied joyfully, just like they did with
Daddy. I said it again, with more energy, as Daddy would.

"Come on and clap those hands for Jesus," I commanded the
people, and they obliged. I followed that with things like "Thank
you, Jesus," "He's worthy of the praise," and "He's a good God." It was
working for a bit, calming my nerves, to hear some of the people in
the crowd shout back their *Hallelujahs* and *Thank you, Jesuses*. I even
heard one of the deacons from behind me cry out, "Let the Lord use
you, young man!"

Once I was calm, I remembered the opening words I'd said in my bedroom. "Give an honor to all the clergymen here tonight," I began in reverence. "The pulpit, the deacons, the ushers, my brother, our head musician, my father and mother, and their special week. It's a privilege to be here tonight."

I took another breath, staring down at my notes on "The Call."

"Can you all please turn with me to Jeremiah, chapter one, please?" As I watched the people flip through their Bibles, I took one last breath and finally began talking through my notes.

"And it reads at verse 4, 'The word of the Lord came to me, saying, before I formed you in the womb I knew you, before you were born, I set you apart, I appointed you a prophet to the nations.'"

I stopped, hearing some of the people shout, "Amen!" They were listening. They were really listening to me. So, I kept on reading what I had written down.

"Verse six says 'Ah, Lord God! Behold, I cannot speak: for I am a child. But the Lord said unto me, say not, I am a child: for thou shalt go to all that I shall send thee, and whatsoever I command thee thou shalt speak. Be not afraid of their faces: for I am with thee to deliver thee, saith the Lord.'"

I closed my Bible, placed my paper on top, and began to speak.

"Saints of God, I want to share with you what I believe God has shared with me. Everyone in here has a destiny. Everyone in here has a purpose. The scripture says that we as Christians, believers of God, are called. God chooses each one of us, handpicked, just like Jeremiah."

Then, just like it happened earlier in my room, my talking slowly turned into preaching the way Daddy sometimes did.

"Here we look at Jeremiah, a young person like you see here in the congregation today. God called him by name to be a prophetic voice over his nation. God had his mind on young Jeremiah, had his chosen path picked out for him from the beginning of time."

I was feeling it, the same feelings Daddy felt when he gave the Word. Zeke began to back me up on the organ with those old-fashioned revival chords he'd talked about. I started singing, reciting all kinds of verses that came to me, and in my mind, it all sounded good.

"Young Jeremiah began to make excuses and questioned God like some of us may have when God has spoken to us. Jeremiah couldn't believe that someone as young as he was at the time could have an encounter with God. It reminds me of the story when God first spoke to Moses at the burning bush, and how he at first didn't believe."

Moses? The burning bush? Where did that come from? It just came out of me, and it was fitting. From what I could hear, I was singing just as good as Zeke could, and preaching like Daddy. In the crowd, some people were dancing, some were shouting, and others were praising God. They were loving it. They really were loving it.

I was up there for about ten more minutes, not remembering half of what I was saying, but proclaiming the word of the Lord. The people were awed and surprised when I finally came to. It seemed that everyone was on their feet, praising God. I looked back at Daddy, who was grinning from ear to ear with joy. Over at the organ, Zeke gave his nod of approval. Mama had tears rolling down her face and was clapping joyfully along with the rest of the crowd. I couldn't believe I did it. I preached for the service—and did a good job.

CHAPTER 20

LOVE FORGIVES ALL WITH A BIG KISS TO SEAL THE DEAL

"Man, Jeremiah, I didn't know you can preach like that!" was the first comment I heard from Roach. He told me that I'd had the whole church in the palm of my hands, preaching and praying like an old deacon. Drew made his way over with Otis as well to tell me I did a great job. Colton decided to take credit for discovering me by telling everyone he was the first to ever hear me give a word.

"I told y'all that he was good," he said. "The best out of all of us."

I was very humbled by the comments, but I was glad that it was all over with. Everyone seemed to enjoy the service tonight, including Rodney. He really hadn't said two words all evening. It wasn't a normal Rodney quiet, thinking of one of his many crazy sayings or names. It was more like a certain humility had come over him. After he told me I did a wonderful job, he then looked straight at Otis.

"Listen, man," he began. "You know I ain't one for all that mushy stuff like everybody else, but I've been thinking a lot about you and Kenny. I feel bad for him being on drugs and things and probably shouldn't have been such a punk about it. I mean, I have two older brothers, and I hope they don't have to go over to Vietnam. I wouldn't know what I would do if one of them went. I guess I'm just trying to say that I'm glad Kenny is alright. I'm glad that you and li'l Sam and your mom have your family back. And I hope you're not mad at me, because, I don't know, I kind of got used to you being with us and everything."

Rodney was seemingly talking in circles, trying his best to apologize. Otis made it easier for him, holding out his hand for a high five. "It's all good, Rodney. I know what you mean, and we still tight."

Rodney let out a huge sigh of relief as he gave Otis a high five. A symbolic peace treaty was settled between the two. Who knew that a church service would change Rodney and make him show some sort of compassion for his friendly rival Otis?

I didn't know if I would ever get up to the podium and give a sermon again, but for my first time, it wasn't so bad. I didn't choke up there. I didn't crack or get all sweaty like I normally would. In fact, I kind of liked preaching. I wouldn't do it every Sunday like Daddy does, but maybe from time to time a bit. However, I knew it was all worth it when I saw Christine and her grandfather walking up.

"Well, well, look who the wind brought us, our old neighbors!" he exclaimed.

"How are you doing, Remington?" Daddy asked with excitement.

"I'm fine, Walter, doing just fine." He then looked at me, still smiling. "This can't be Jeremiah McGill," he said. "You've grown up a lot since the last time I saw you. I remember you being a little something with glasses that were bigger than your face, and now you're becoming a nice young man. Preached the whole house down tonight, didn't you?"

"Yes, sir," I replied.

"Well, I think it's wonderful, just wonderful to see you up there," he approved. "You look very handsome, and seem very well-mannered, too."

"Thank you, sir."

As Mr. Remington and Daddy began talking about old times, I waited beside them with Christine. She looked at me and I looked at her. When she smiled, it was like this fresh sweet savoring aroma engulfed her. It smelled like fresh sugar cookies.

"You did very good up there tonight," she said.

"Thanks," I said, trying to summon my manly person.

I didn't say anything else, trying not to ruin the mood. Just having her beside me, I felt myself melting. At last, I brought myself to talk to her some more.

"Christine, I'm really glad you came tonight," I said.

"Me too," she agreed. "Grandpa really had a good time. He said he may come back and visit again."

"That's great. He looked happy." I looked down at my black shoes, a bit reserved about the next thing I was going to say. "Christine, I know that Rodney claimed to like you for a bit and everything. But I always liked you, a lot."

"Why didn't you say anything, Jeremiah?"

"I don't know . . . I guess I didn't know if you'd want to like someone like me."

"I always liked you, Jeremiah."

"Really?" I felt my head pop up, attentive to her.

"Sure I did, ever since we used to be neighbors a long time ago."

"Well, gee, I didn't know that. I mean, I think we'd go good together and all. And you came and had a wonderful time tonight. I was wondering if we could, you know, only if you want to . . ."

In the midst of me trying to get my words out, Christine looked around us. When she figured no one was looking, it happened. She leaned over while I was talking and kissed me on the cheek. She literally kissed me. I wondered if anyone saw it. My response wasn't words but instead laughter that sounded exactly like Goofy. I was kind of embarrassed, but she thought it was the cutest thing in the world.

A lot has changed in my life. Some good, some bad. I remember Daddy asking me a question, back around a year ago. He asked me if I knew what I was called to do. I didn't know what he meant. Now, I got it.

When Christine left with Mr. Remington, she waved delicately at me. Watching her leave, I still couldn't believe she'd kissed me on the cheek. I knew one thing—I wasn't gonna wash that cheek for a long time after that.

AUTHOR BIO — JOSEPH L. MOORE

MG author Joseph L. Moore has been a storyteller since childhood. His inspiration comes from listening to his parents and their friends on Sunday evenings talk about their times growing up in the church as young kids, their joy reminiscing, and the adventures they had. Joseph wanted to share their rich history and has woven that into his new young adult coming of age novel, *The Call of Jeremiah McGill*, a historical fiction story with a Christian backdrop.

Joseph believes a good book is one with honesty, that shares the truth of a situation whether good or bad, and one where the reader can find themselves in the story. In *The Call of Jeremiah McGill*, a young boy is discovering who he is called to be in life. Joseph hopes his young readers come away from his book learning a bit about history and asking questions about Jesus and their own spirituality, and that it starts a conversation that lasts long after the book is closed.

When he isn't writing spiritual and enlightening books for young adults, Joseph is a musician and singer and enjoys listening to soft worship music as he writes. Having grown up in the church and in faith, Joseph currently serves as a minister of music of House of Prayer, World Outreach Mission. An educator for nine years, Joseph lives in Cape Girardeau, Missouri, south of St. Louis. *The Call of Jeremiah McGill* is his debut novel.

Made in the USA
Middletown, DE
22 January 2023